The Victor

To Sara!.
Freemasonry Never looked
So Sexy!.

Love
Nicole
xx

ACKNOWLEDGEMENTS

Many people grow up around various organizations. Some grow up around military, I grew up around Freemasonry. I have so many great memories of my dad getting dressed in a dinner suit or tails looking so handsome. I never asked what he did all I knew was - he was going to Lodge. It all seemed so mysterious. I loved that aspect of it all.

This series is not an expose on the workings of Freemasonry nor will any secrets be revealed. But my heroes in this series are Freemasons. They're proud men and proud of everything Freemasonry stands for and does for the community, because in reality they do a lot.

There are a few people who helped with getting my first self published title off the ground.

Firstly to my editor Belinda Holmes who cracked her whip and told me my characters needed some work. Thanks B, we got them there. One day we will sit down to a glass of goon.

Laura Gibson of Aletheia Designs who designed my fabulous cover. Thanks for always being cheerful when I battered you with text messages or emails.

To my wonderful friends Shey, Rachael, Sasha, Sara, Heather B and Heather L. The Bookworm girls and every single person who comments on my Facebook page or tweets with me. Thanks for making this job so very special.

To S and Z you've got to stop growing. Keep believing and you will be amazing.

On the front cover of this book is a unique logo. That logo was designed by my wonderful husband Jason. Babe, thank you for your unfailing belief in me and the constant support you give and for using your out of this world artistic skills in creating my logo. Love you!

To the two Freemasons in my life: my wonderful husband, Jason and my amazing father, Denis.

And to the Freemasons around the world. Especially the members of the Lodges of the Grand Lodge of Scotland of Western Australia.

CHAPTER 1

Ava Vaughan-Jacobs smoothed down her emerald green dress and adjusted her diamond and emerald earrings. She probably shouldn't wear Cole's wedding gift when she was about to ask him for a divorce. Whether it was in bad taste or not, she had her own reasons for wearing them. Even though she wanted to end their marriage, the earrings had been given to her when a new chapter of her life was starting. She hoped tonight would be a new start too. It seemed fitting to wear them.

Would Cole notice the earrings or not? Would he wonder why she had them on? Remember when and where he'd given them to her?

Stop it! She told herself. None of it mattered. All that mattered was when she returned to her room, she'd have Cole's agreement for a divorce.

With one last look in the mirror, she picked up her purse and checked it for her phone and room key. She'd decided to stay at the hotel instead of driving the three and half hours it would take to get back to the house in Margaret River. The time had come to get on with her life. Even if it did mean divorcing the man who still consumed ninety percent of her thoughts. No matter how hard she'd tried over the last six months to forget Cole Jacobs, he still invaded her dreams every night. A clean break was the only way to break the cycle. While still living in a house owned by Cole, her connection to him would always be strong. After she'd asked him for a divorce, she would take off the beautiful wedding set he'd given her and move out of the place that had provided her with sanctuary to heal after the loss she'd suffered.

While approaching Cole at this charity event may not seem the best way of asking for what she wanted, for her there was safety in numbers. She knew he was conscious of how the public perceived him at events. Especially after a woman he had been seeing created a scene at an important business function. Her actions had almost cost him a major account. As this particular charity was one of his family's favorite ones, there was no way he'd do anything to cause a scene and bring unnecessary attention to his them.

Taking a deep, cleansing breath, she opened the door and exited her room. Hopefully, when she returned she would have Cole's agreement and she could leave the last year behind her.

The noise from the ballroom drifted toward her as she rounded the corner. She'd timed her arrival for a half hour after the official start time. Not that anyone arrived at these events on time. It was all about creating an entrance for some people. Not her. Ava preferred to slip in with minimal fuss. Something that had been impossible to achieve when she and Cole had started dating, and later, during the short time they actually lived together after saying their wedding vows. Every time she'd walked into a restaurant, or an event similar to this one, she'd felt everyone looking at her. Judging her for trying to be something she had no hope of being.

Before she started seeing Cole she had been a university graduate trying to find a job in the cutthroat event planning world. An unremarkable girl with an unremarkable background, she was so out of her league with Cole. She'd always worried she'd run into an ex-lover of his. She'd seen him in the society pages with beautiful women. How would she ever match up to those women?

She wasn't that same girl anymore. Time on her own had made her stronger. Able to face any situation headfirst and not back down from what she wanted or who she'd become.

Ava entered the lavishly decorated ballroom, noting the blue and silver tones of the tablecloths and table settings. The lights glowed on the silverware. Women were standing around wearing the finest gowns and the finest jewels. Looking like they owned half the city. Some of them probably did. It had a distinct, sophisticated feel about it. And for a moment, all the insecurities she'd thought she'd overcome hit her with the force of a gale force wind. In her off-the-rack gown, she knew she didn't fit in. Her earrings, though beautiful, were no match for what adorned the ears of many women in the room.

No matter how strong she thought she had become, the truth of the matter was she would never be a part of Cole's world. Stepping into this room reinforced her resolve to ask him for a divorce.

A waiter carrying a tray of assorted drinks stopped in front of her. She helped herself to a glass of champagne and took a sip. The tartness hit the back of her throat. She took another large swallow, building up the courage to begin looking for Cole.

She started a slow walk around the room, hating being partnerless. The last time she'd been alone at one of these events she'd met Cole.

Ava closed her eyes against the memories peppering her brain. How Cole had rescued her from the octopus hands of a drunken guest. It had taken one smile and she'd been lost. She should've run that night. Run as far away as possible. If she had, she would've saved herself from a world of heartache.

Enough, she commanded herself. Over the last few months she'd done plenty of thinking and planning. After tonight she would put the plans in motion. Surely Cole would agree that it would be pointless for them to remain married. He would relish having his freedom again. Who knows, maybe he already had another woman warming his bed. It wouldn't surprise her. Cole had always been a player. The longest he'd stayed with a woman before her had been three months. It seemed that five months into their relationship Cole had started to slowly draw away from her. Telling her he had to attend more Lodge Drysor meetings. She'd never asked him about his Freemason dealings, as much as she'd wanted to. She'd heard all about the secrecy surrounding the society. What happened behind closed doors had always intrigued her. But she'd respected the history behind Freemasonry, so she never pressured him to tell her what went on at his meetings.

Problem was, she hadn't believed he'd been attending those meetings. Her conviction that she wasn't enough of a woman to keep Cole interested ate away at her. Undermining the basis of their relationship. Even when they went to functions together, women flirted outrageously around him. Why wouldn't he be tempted? Eventually she'd persuaded herself he was cheating on her.

Then she'd taken the test that had changed everything.

She'd heard the gossip around the social circles that she'd trapped him with a baby. That he was only marrying her out of obligation. Cole had assured her she hadn't trapped him, but still he hadn't told her he loved her. He'd told her he cared deeply for her. She tried to accept he was the type of guy who didn't express his feelings. Couldn't say the words every woman hoped to hear.

"You shouldn't be standing alone. Not at event like this. Perhaps I can help you find your table?"

Ava turned and came face to face with a handsome man in a tuxedo. Any other woman would flutter their eyelashes and smile coyly at him. For her, she'd only ever wanted one man in a tuxedo. And this man wasn't him.

"Thank you, but I'm fine. I'm looking for someone."

As far as brush-offs went, it was gentle. Fortunately the man took the hint.

"I hope you find whoever it is you're looking for."

Ava smiled and turned back to survey the room. The crowd had increased since she'd arrived. Trying to find Cole would be even harder now. But she was determined to find him.

Whatever it took, she would walk out of this room with his agreement for a divorce.

Cole Jacobs listened with one ear as his mother talked to him about the near disaster with the florist. He was missing an important meeting with his friends and fellow Freemasons, Dominic, Jude and Declan, to be here this evening. They were planning the next move for their charity. Things were heating up and care needed to be taken so what they hoped to accomplish wasn't exposed. One false move and many lives could be lost.

"Cole, are you listening to me?"

He leaned in and kissed his mum on the cheek. She'd been lonely since Dad had passed away four months ago. He was glad she had her charities to keep her busy. He worried about her, though, and always made sure if she needed him, he was there for her.

"Sorry, Mum. I've got a few things on my mind."

"Is she one of them?" His spine stiffened when he looked over to where Mum pointed. His elusive wife stood not ten feet away from him. The wife who hadn't bothered to stand by his side when his father had died. The wife who had walked out when their relationship had hit a troubled patch. The wife who'd ignored that he was hurting as much as she was.

"What the hell is she doing here? She wasn't invited."

"Cole." Mum's tone said it all.

"Sorry, Mum."

"You need to do something about this marriage of yours. It's not healthy to live apart."

Cole blew out a frustrated breath. "It's a bit difficult when she refuses to speak to me."

"You should've gone and seen her. Tried harder to communicate with her." Mum looked at him shrewdly. "Unless you didn't want to in case she said something you didn't want to hear."

Cole had no plans to let his mum know it suited him to have Ava safely ensconced in his Margaret River property, and not someplace else where he couldn't keep her safe. She was far enough away from his and Lodge Drysor's dealings, but not far enough away he couldn't get to her if he needed to. The less she knew the safer she would remain.

Now he had the added job of dealing with his father's estate and making sure the company continued to be profitable, as well as making sure the transition from his father's management style to his went smoothly. Chasing after Ava got pushed back in his mind.

"I've been busy over the last couple of months, Mum."

"Still, no matter how busy Dad was, he always put you and me first."

The last thing he needed was a lecture. Nor did he want to mention that that hadn't always been the case with Dad. Besides, he needed to find out why Ava was at a function where she definitely wasn't on the guest list.

"I'm sorry to leave you, Mum, but—" he looked toward where Ava stood. She still hadn't seen him but he could tell she was looking for someone. Him, perhaps?

"Go. It's fine. Although Cole...?"

He turned back to his mum. "Yes."

"I don't know what happened, but remember she's your wife and where you are. Try not to be the hard-headed person I know you can be."

He chuckled. "Yes Mum." He gave her another quick kiss on the cheek and made his way to where Ava stood.

Everything he'd felt over the last couple of months bubbled to the surface. He'd expected she would attend his father's funeral. It wasn't like she didn't know when and where it was being held. He'd phoned and left a message for her, hating that he couldn't tell her personally, talk to her. He would've driven down but he couldn't leave his mum. She'd been devastated when his father died. He had been worried she would have an emotional breakdown. He'd been torn between the duty of the son and husband. Her non-attendance at the funeral told Cole all he needed to know. It shattered everything he thought he knew about her; every hope he'd had that they could rebuild what they'd had between them died the moment his father's coffin had been lowered into the ground.

Drawing on the anger and hurt and disappointment he'd felt that day, Cole walked up behind Ava, unable to stop the memories of the first night he'd met her blasting his brain the closer he got to her. How badly he'd wanted to knock out the guy who'd had his hands all over her when he could tell Ava wanted nothing to do with the man. How she'd thanked him for rescuing her. He'd been captivated by her freshness and innocence from that moment on.

Cole tamped down on those thoughts. He couldn't let himself recall that time. It had become the past the moment she'd devalued their relationship by walking out on him. Not trusting him enough to care and look after her. But Ava was here, when she hadn't made any attempt to contact him for months. Her making the first move had to mean something, a door opening for them to communicate through. Maybe they could find a way to put the past hurts behind them and try again.

"Ava."

She whirled around quickly. He took a step back so he didn't get splashed with champagne. He took in the surprise on her face, as if she hadn't expected to see him there. He didn't quite believe it. After all this time of hiding away, she showed up at his mum's favorite charity event? No, she wanted something. Finding out what she wanted and getting rid of her with a minimum of fuss was what he needed to do. No matter that seeing her again made his heart beat faster than normal. Her dress clung to her curves, accentuating her luscious breasts. His eyes roved over the face he hadn't seen in months, taking in the way her green eyes glittered brightly. Then he saw them. The earrings. The wedding gift he'd given her. The hope he'd had when he'd bought them for her. Cole clenched his fists tightly to stop from reaching out to touch them.

He repeated the sentiment he'd uttered when his mum directed his attention to where Ava had been standing. "What the hell are you doing here?"

Ava stared into the dark brown depths of Cole's eyes. A hardness she'd never seen before replaced the softness that had always been there when he'd looked at her.

"I, uh," she cleared her throat. She could do this. She could talk to him. "I've come to see you."

He crossed his arms, the fabric of his suit jacket pulling tight across his shoulders. "Really," he drawled. "Aren't you a little late?"

"What do you mean?"

As Cole took a step closer to her, the musky scent of his cologne wafted over her. Memories crashed down on her. Memories of that scent surrounding her as he'd made love to her. She'd loved walking into the bathroom and inhaling the scent after he'd showered. He didn't know she'd taken one of his t-shirts and had sprayed his cologne on it when she'd walked out of their marital home. She'd slept with that t-shirt for weeks after she'd left him.

"I mean, the time to come and see me would've been when I *needed* to have my wife by my side." He paused, before continuing, "The day I buried my father."

Ava opened her mouth to tell him she'd been there. At the back of the crowd, wearing a big black hat so no one would see her. She'd wanted to go up to him the moment she'd seen him. To slip her hand in his and give him all the support he'd needed. But her courage had failed. Before anyone had seen her she'd snuck away. Her heart breaking even more seeing the despair on his face as they lowered his father's casket into the ground

They'd been living apart for months. Communication spasmodic. She'd missed his call to let her know his father had died. She'd heard the pain and devastation in his voice. She'd wanted to rush up to Perth then and there to be with him. Give him some strength, but after she'd continually pushed him aside when she'd been lost in her depression about losing their baby, she didn't know if she had the right.

"I'm sorry." Such inadequate words, but she had to say something to him.

"Your sympathy is touching, albeit a bit late."

Ava looked around and saw they were drawing attention to themselves. Which wasn't surprising considering they hadn't been seen together since that awful time when they were photographed leaving the hospital. Even at the lowest point in her life, the press still managed to hound her and Cole. Cole had been furious and if she hadn't almost collapsed when he'd let her go, she had no doubt he would've got into a fight with the sleazy photographer.

"Cole, can we go somewhere private and talk?"

"Now she wants to talk," he muttered.

"Please, Cole?" She inwardly cringed at the pleading tone in her voice.

"If you hadn't noticed," he paused and looked at the crowd around them. "Now's not a good time to have a talk of any sort. Why don't you ring the office and arrange an appointment."

"*An appointment?*" Ava tightened her hold on her champagne glass to stop from throwing the remaining contents in Cole's face.

Cole leaned forward, his eyes looking even harder than they had before. "If you were my wife in the true sense of the word, we wouldn't be having this conversation. We'd be in this room talking with friends. Instead you turn up as if we haven't been living apart for six months. So yes, Ava, call my assistant and make an appointment."

He started to turn away but she grabbed his arm, ignoring the jolt of awareness between them.

Ava opened her mouth and then closed it again. Not sure if she could form the words she needed to form. She'd always believed when she married it would last a lifetime. She thought Cole would be her lifetime partner. If only they'd waited and not rushed into marriage. Would things have turned out differently then?

"I have to go, Ava."

She fixed her gaze on a spot over his left shoulder and blurted out what she'd come here to say. "I want a divorce."

CHAPTER 2

Cole sat at the bar, empty glass in his hand. As much as he wanted another shot, after doing three in quick succession it probably wasn't a good idea.

I want a divorce.

No amount of vodka was going to drown out the sound of those words. It certainly wasn't what he expected Ava to say when she told him she wanted to *talk*.

He'd told her, "No," and walked away. He didn't want to know what she did after that. She hadn't stayed at the fundraiser.

"Can I join you?"

He placed the empty glass down on the bar and turned to face Ava. He noted that she'd changed out of the dress she'd been wearing earlier. The jeans she had on looked soft and well worn. They hugged her legs. Her soft sweater dipped at the neckline and he glimpsed the cleavage he'd enjoyed on many occasions. He folded his arms across his chest, suppressing the urge to reach out and pull her close. Convince her that divorce wasn't the only option for them.

Although, he had no desire to talk to her either. He just wanted to be left alone so he could think. Plan out his next move.

"Do you really think I want to talk to you?"

"I don't care what you want or think." Ava said, as she ignored the leave-me-the-fuck-alone vibe he gave off and sat on the barstool next to him. He turned back toward the bar and signaled the bartender, who came over promptly.

"What can I get you both?"

Cole raised his glass, indicating he wanted another shot.

"I'll have a club soda, please."

Waiting until their drinks sat in front of them, Cole looked over at Ava. She played with the straw in her drink. Twirling it around, making the ice clink against the glass.

They sat in silence for a few more moments, his gaze returning to the contents of his drink. A drink he didn't want or need. Out of the corner of his eye he could see Ava's agitation growing.

"Cole, I'm sorry."

Fuck it. I need this drink.

He lifted his glass and downed the contents in one swallow. He carefully placed his empty glass back on the bar and swiveled again so that he brushed her knees with his. "What exactly are you *sorry* about, Ava? Sorry for walking out when I was hurting as much as you? Sorry for not being by my side while I buried my father? Or sorry for asking me for a divorce when I'm about to face a roomful of people? I'd really like to know."

Her eyes had widened with every word he spoke. In the muted light of the bar he could almost convince himself he could see remorse in her eyes. But she'd known exactly what was happening at this hotel tonight. She'd known what she planned to say to him.

"I, uh, I," she stopped and took a sip of her drink. "I thought it was time."

"Really?" he drawled. "You thought it was time. After six months of avoiding my calls, not answering my emails, you decided tonight was the night."

"Okay, so maybe tonight wasn't the best place to talk to you."

"You think?"

"No need to be a smart ass, Cole."

He laughed harshly. "Did you honestly think I would be all sweetness and light about this?"

"I'd hoped you would've been more reasonable about things."

"Baby, I stopped being reasonable," he flicked back his shirt cuff and looked at his watch. "About five hours ago."

In the back of his mind Cole knew he was being the asshole she called him. He never let his emotions get the better of him. He had a reputation for his cool head in uncomfortable situations. Tonight, after her request for a divorce, he relinquished his normal ironclad control over his emotions and let them run free.

"Fine. I'll call your office and make an appointment like you asked me to." Ava stood to go. Her leg knocked his and heat shot through him. His body stirred to life at her touch. He couldn't let her go without tasting her again.

Cole reached out and wrapped his fingers around her wrist, halting her departure.

"What?" she demanded. "You got what you wanted."

"No I haven't." Cole stood and tugged her until she was flush against him. His body relished having Ava close again. Without thinking what he was doing, he placed his hands on either side of her face, tilting her head up.

"Cole?" she whispered, as he closed the gap and took possession of her slightly parted lips.

At the first touch and taste of her, recollections he'd pushed deep into the far recesses of his mind came forward, reminding him of what they'd once shared. As Ava opened her mouth beneath his, everything around him faded. All he concentrated on was the woman in his arms.

His wife.

She tasted sweet. A hint of strawberry from her lip balm and a lingering tartness from the slice of lemon in her club soda mingled together to entice him. He pulled her closer. Her body fit perfectly against his. He sunk his fingers into her silky tresses, remembering how her hair had felt brushing his skin as they'd made love. She moaned and his body responded immediately.

He'd fooled himself into thinking he could be happy without her in his life. How wrong he'd been. Holding her again only reinforced how much he wanted her. He wanted to drag her upstairs and take her over and over again. It had been too long since they'd shared a bed. Would Ava be open to spending the night with him if he suggested it? It seemed so. It was probably the worst thing for them to do after not seeing each other for so long. But it also could be the right thing too.

No.

He needed to think with his head, not his dick.

Cole pulled his lips away from Ava's, keeping his arms loosely around her waist. Plans needed to be made. But before he started planning, he had something to say to Ava.

"Divorce is not an option."

Ava had forgotten how dangerous Cole could be when he held her close. How one touch from his lips had her forgetting the hurt they'd put each other through. One touch had her recalling the romantic dinners. The surprise gifts he gave her. They'd had good times before everything fell apart.

Slowly her fuzzy brain cleared and his words resounded loudly in her mind.

Divorce is not an option.

She took two steps back and wrapped her arms around her middle. He couldn't mean that? Could he? Oh, she knew he'd said no when she first asked him, but couldn't he see they were better apart than together? He could move on, find a more suitable woman for him. Someone who suited the demands of his high society life better than her.

"What do you mean? I want a divorce, Cole. Don't you think it would be best for the both of us if we ended our marriage?"

His jaw tightened with every word she spoke. The steely glint of hardness returned to his eyes. A shiver rippled down her spine. He'd always looked at her with affection or desire. She wasn't used to this hardness directed at her.

"No, I don't think it's time." He pulled his smartphone out of his pocket. He swiped at the screen then looked back at her. "Meet me at my office tomorrow morning at ten o'clock. We can discuss it then."

"I thought you told me I had to ring your *assistant* to make an appointment?"

He shrugged his shoulders. "Now I'm telling you I can see you at ten."

"Well, I'm sorry, that doesn't work for me." She had nowhere she had to be tomorrow. But Cole didn't need to know that. No way was she going to fall at his feet just because he'd decided he could meet her.

Cole stepped forward and placed a hand on her cheek. It took everything in her not place her hand over his. To deepen the skin to skin contact between them. "Whatever you have planned, cancel it. It's then or it's not at all." He leaned forward and kissed the tip of her nose, before letting his hand fall to his side. "Your choice, sweetheart."

There was no affection in the endearment, only a hint of irony. Ava knew if she wanted to get the discussion of a divorce happening, she would have to go and see Cole tomorrow.

"Fine, I'll see you at your office tomorrow." She turned to walk away, only to stop after a couple of steps. "But don't think because we're meeting in your office that you're going to talk me out of this. I will get what I want, Cole."

"We'll see."

Ava opened her mouth to argue and then closed it. It would be better to save her arguments for tomorrow. She had a feeling she was going to need everything within her to resist Cole.

As she walked out of the bar, conscious of Cole watching her retreating back, one thought drummed through her mind. She should've got a lawyer.

CHAPTER 3

Ava wiped her hands down her navy dress. She stood out the front of Cole's building. Waiting until exactly 10.00 a.m. before she walked in. He may have thought he'd won the battle last night. It didn't mean she would bend to his will.

As the alarm she'd programmed into her phoned chimed, she took a deep breath and walked through the sliding glass doors.

She'd been into Cole's building numerous times. The black marble floors gleamed, looking like they'd recently been refinished and polished. A new, more welcoming security desk replaced the previous utilitarian desk that had been situated in the middle of the double story foyer. She looked up and noticed a beautiful chandelier suspended from the ceiling.

An air of sophistication cloaked the building, something that hadn't been there before. The plastics business must be doing well. Before she'd left Cole, the business had been in a bit of a slump. In addition to his endless meetings with Lodge Drysor, he had been putting in long hours in the office. Well, so he told her. Many a time he'd come home and there had been a hint of flowery perfume clinging to his jacket. He'd always denied he'd been with someone else. She had trouble believing him, especially knowing that before her, he had a reputation as a major player around town.

"Ava? Is that you?"

She whirled and came face to face with Dominic Cacciari, one of Cole's good friends and a member of Cole's Lodge. "Hi Dominic. How are you?"

He leaned in and kissed her cheek. "It's good to see you. How have you been?"

His question seemed innocent, but Ava had been around Dominic enough times to know it was anything but. He was evaluating. Like he always did. Determining what the situation between her and Cole really was. Had Cole spoken to him? Did Dominic know she'd asked for a divorce? Did Dominic even know about what happened between her and Cole? He'd become one of the most successful businessmen in Australia, not to mention the Master of Lodge Drysor, by being astute and sizing up his competition.

"I'm good, thanks. Just heading up to see Cole."

"Hmm, he did say you were coming to see him today." He paused as if assessing what he wanted to say next. He looked at her and she felt like she was about to be scolded by her parents. "Things have been difficult and stressful for him recently. Bear that in mind when you talk to him."

Ava took a step back. "Are you trying to warn me off, Dominic? Because things haven't exactly been easy for me either."

"I never said they were," he responded mildly, before flicking his shirt cuff back and looking at his watch. "I have to go. It was good to see you, Ava. I hope to see you again…with Cole."

As he walked off, Ava wondered what just happened. Dominic had always been a gentleman to her. Always friendly. He'd never talked to her as brusquely as he'd just done.

Had Cole discussed their problems with him? Was this how she should expect to be treated by all of Cole's friends now? She supposed if she had a group of close girlfriends they'd be icy toward Cole. It didn't mean she liked being treated like an outcast. Cole had been to blame for their marriage breakdown too. He'd let her run. He hadn't fought for her.

She strode over to the bank of elevators, stabbing at the button, replaying the conversation with Dominic the whole ride up to the top floor. As the doors opened she came face to face with the man in question. Ava opened her mouth to fire off her questions at him.

Cole held up his hand. "Whatever you're about to say, say it in my office."

He grabbed her hand and turned toward his office. The urge to dig her heels into the plush carpet overwhelmed her. She didn't appreciate him cutting her off. She also knew creating a scene in front of his staff would not impress him. Ava needed to walk out of this meeting with him agreeing to a divorce. Regardless of him telling her last night that it wasn't an option.

As soon as the door closed, she pulled her hand away from his and crossed her arms over her chest.

"Can I talk now?"

Cole leaned against his desk, mirroring her crossed arm pose. She sucked in a breath as his shirt stretched across his chest. Last night she'd been pressed against that chest. During their time apart it seemed to have got harder. Like it always had, the moment he'd closed his arms around her, she'd felt safe. She'd always felt safe in his arms.

Ava gave herself a mental shake. Getting lost in memories would be the worst possible thing she could do with him. She would more than likely agree to anything he said. When Cole centered his attention solely on her; saying no became impossible.

"Forgot what you wanted to say?"

Cole's voice broke through her thoughts, bringing her back to the present, his sarcasm reigniting her indignation.

"What have you been telling your friends?"

"I don't know what you're talking about."

"Really? I got *warned* by Dominic that I should bear in mind things have been stressful for you recently." She took a step closer to Cole and stabbed a finger in his chest. "So I ask you again, what have you been saying to your friends?"

Cole grabbed her hand and pressed it against his chest, making it impossible for her to move away. "I haven't said anything."

Ava tried to pull away, only to have Cole tighten his grip. "I don't think I believe you."

Cole finally released her and went to stand by the window. Had her words hurt him? It didn't seem likely. Nothing she said could hurt him. Cole kept his emotions on a tight, short leash. Even when she lay in the hospital bed, mourning the loss of their baby, he'd stoically held her hand. Assuring her that everything would be okay. But it hadn't been. Whenever he'd tried to talk, she'd always shut him down. He never once lost his temper with her. Sometimes she wanted him to let go of his control. In her state of depression, she'd rationalized if Cole argued with her, he cared for her. Still wanted her. With his quiet acceptance of her closing herself off from him, she took it as a sign he had stopped caring and wanted her out of his life.

Leaving her to attend Lodge Drysor meetings she could cope with, to a degree. Sometimes the secrecy surrounding the organization annoyed her. Why a group of men had to have secrets always intrigued her. She respected the principle of Freemasonry. However, when she'd been deep in her depression, it had hurt when Cole kept that part of his life away from her.

When he'd started leaving to go to work dinners without her, she knew it was only a matter of time before he started looking elsewhere for pleasure. Before they'd married he'd taken her everywhere with him. She'd been proud to be his partner. After their wedding and her miscarriage it seemed like he didn't want to have anything to do with her. He never tried very hard to convince her to join him.

"Have I ever lied to you, Ava?"

She turned to face him. "I don't know, Cole. Maybe."

He gave no outward indication her words struck a chord. But his face took on the hard mask again. She didn't like it. Knowing she caused it didn't sit well with her. But it didn't matter. Soon they would be going their separate ways and he could find someone he really loved. Not someone he'd felt obliged to marry because she'd fallen pregnant.

"When have I *ever* given you any reason to think I've lied to you?"

"Does it matter? Our marriage is over, Cole. Surely you have to agree. We've been living apart for six months. And the months prior to me moving out weren't exactly what a newly married couple should've been experiencing."

"It wasn't my choice to be living apart. You ran away, Ava. You were the one who walked out on our marriage. Not me. I was, no, I am, committed to the vows we made that day. This is why I'm not going to agree to a divorce."

Ava clenched her fists in frustration. She didn't want to fight with Cole. Couldn't he see she was doing this for him? Why was he being so difficult? Why couldn't he give her what she wanted?

"Why, Cole? This doesn't make any sense. What do you want from me?"

Cole walked toward Ava. Residual anger at her comments about believing he lied to her lingered within him. He'd never lied to her. Well, that wasn't entirely true. There were some things happening with Lodge Drysor that she couldn't know about, so technically people would probably say he had lied to her. He just didn't agree with them. He hadn't lied about what he felt for her. He cared deeply for her. Had been devastated when they'd lost their baby. He'd been so excited to be a father. The first time they'd heard their baby's heartbeat had been the second best day of his life. The first had been marrying her. He wasn't planning on letting Ava go just yet.

It was time to set the plan in motion to get what he wanted.

"It's quite simple, Ava. I want you. It's time you moved back in with me. To our home. Our bedroom. It's time for us to be husband and wife again."

Emotions played across her face; anger, disbelief and yearning. The last one fleeting, but it gave him hope she wanted to give their marriage a second chance.

"What is this going to achieve, Cole? What has changed between now and then?"

"A lot has changed. Time has eased the pain of our loss, hasn't it?"

"For you maybe. But there's not a day that goes by where I don't wonder *what if*. We would be parents now if things had turned out differently. I see women with babies in prams and I ache because that should've been me. It should've been *us*." Her hands covered her face and she whispered. "It should've been us, Cole."

Cole scraped his fingers down his face. He hadn't forgotten. He'd had Ava's due date highlighted in his diary and on his smartphone. He hadn't wanted to delete the reminder because he hadn't wanted to forget. He didn't know how he got through that day when it arrived. Somehow, he had. What had Ava done the day their child was supposed to have been born? He'd wanted to go see her. He knew she'd be upset and he'd wanted to hold her. Comfort her. Everything she'd denied him when they'd lost their baby. He'd done all he could at the time, stayed stoic and strong. Taken the necessary steps when hell was breaking loose. But after she'd started shutting him out...

He'd wanted to go see her. He should have.

Could he really be angry with her for not attending his father's funeral when he hadn't gone to her? Both of them had made so many mistakes.

The loss of their baby was something they needed to talk about. They'd avoided it for so long.

Was she ready now to listen and discuss?

"I know," he said quietly. "I haven't forgotten I could be holding my son or daughter now."

Ava turned away from him, her spine rigid and unforgiving. "I don't want to talk about this."

He sighed. He shouldn't have hoped that maybe this time was different. Ava always put the barriers up when uncomfortable subjects came up. He could push her but he didn't see the point. Not when his main focus was to get her back into their house.

Cole decided on a different tack. He had worked out a reason for them to spend more time together. He knew even if he could persuade her to move back in with him, she would do everything she could to avoid spending time with him. The two months after her miscarriage she'd spent most of the time in a different part of the house. Had moved into another suite of rooms, saying she needed space.

He hadn't recognized the signs as a form of depression that had taken hold of Ava. Instead of letting her stay away from him that first night, he should've picked her up and taken her back to their bedroom. If he had, perhaps they wouldn't be in this situation now.

So many *should haves* and *what ifs*.

"I've got a proposition for you," he stated.

She turned around and faced him, surprise etched over her face at the sudden change of subject. "A proposition?"

"Yes. I want you to work with me on a project. I need your event planning skills for an event Lodge Drysor is putting on in March. It's important to all of us that it's a success."

Ava didn't know what to make of Cole's proposition. She hadn't realized Cole knew that her event planning business had really taken off over the last three months, after she'd landed the account for a national surf shop franchise. The company had rebranded their logo and the parties she'd arranged in each state had been a big success and had increased the profitability of the franchise.

Her immediate response was no. Why would she want to spend time with Cole when she wanted to end their marriage? Working with the Lodge, however, was a different story. It would be a way to find out if there was more to his Lodge and their meetings than he'd told her. Maybe she'd even be able to go to a meeting and see what they did. Whenever he'd gone to a meeting, dressed in his black dinner suit, her heart had skipped a beat and she couldn't wait for him to return so she could peel the suit off.

"I'm not saying I can do it." She kept her tone casual. "But what is it you want me to do?"

He pointed to where two couches were situated by the window. "Why don't we sit down and I'll get some coffee and we can discuss it."

It was then she noticed some papers already laid out on the squat coffee table between the two couches.

"You planned this, didn't you? This meeting was never about discussing our divorce."

"When I told you to come here last night, it was to talk about your need for a divorce. It wasn't until later that the idea to talk to you about this event struck me."

"What did you do, Cole? Fire the person you'd lined up for the job first thing this morning? I don't need pity jobs, thank you very much."

"Please Ava. Come and sit down so we can talk about this."

She sighed, knowing Cole wasn't going to let her leave until she'd listened to him. She knew he could be a hardheaded businessman. She'd just never had it directed at her. Ava walked over to the couch and sat, reaching out to pick up a couple of papers off the table.

From what she could tell, the event appeared to be pretty much all planned out. The gala was going to take place at one of the largest hotels in the city. It was a fundraiser for the Parklite Foundation. A charity she'd never heard of. Then again, she didn't know all the charities around the city. She thought Cole and his friends would support one of the major well-known charities, like the Salvation Army or Cancer Research.

Cole sat down next to her, his spicy scent drifting toward her. She closed her eyes, inhaled deeply, remembering being held in his arms.

"So what do you think?" he asked.

Her eyes snapped open, heat rushing though her. She focused her attention back on the papers in front of her. "I think you don't need me at all. What's really happening here, Cole? And why me? There are better qualified event planners than me in this town."

"It's quite simple, really. I did not fire the planner at all. He had to pull out due to an unexpected illness. We now find ourselves in need of someone to take over and follow through on our vision. But we weren't happy with what he'd come up with anyway. If he hadn't terminated the contract, it's likely we would've dismissed him. As for the why you, why not? We need an event planner and seeing as you're one, it makes perfect sense to ask you."

"More convenient than making perfect sense."

Cole shrugged his shoulders. "Maybe. The issue is if he'd told us he was ill before Christmas we could've arranged something. The invites were supposed to go out the first week of January. We've only just found out that they weren't sent. They haven't even been designed yet."

"And did you know about this last night when we talked?"

"Yes, but as I said, it wasn't until after I'd left the bar that I thought you would be perfect for the job."

Her business mind told to her to take the job, knowing that it would look fantastic on her resume to have another big name listed. Not to mention give a boost to her bank account when she needed it the most. Her heart screamed at her to run as far away as she could. Taking the job would mean she'd probably have to work closely with Cole. She'd come here to get a divorce, not get drawn back under his spell. Ava knew the more time she spent with Cole, the more she'd want to stay with him.

Ava had to think about her future and Cole could play no part of it. If he'd cared or wanted her at all, he would've come to see her. Tried to get her back.

And the phone calls and emails, didn't they tell you he was trying? You chose to ignore his efforts. Or here's a thought, you could've gone to see him.

She hated that voice in her head when it was being reasonable.

"I don't think this is a good idea, Cole. Thank you for thinking of me but I'm afraid you're going to have to find someone else for the job."

"Take this job and I'll give you a quick, easy divorce. Don't take the job and I drag you through the courts for months. Your choice, Ava."

CHAPTER 4

What would she say? The last thing he would give her would be a divorce. But he knew if he threw that in she might agree to the job. He'd seen the work she'd done for the surf franchise. He knew she would be able to bring exactly what they needed for the Parklite Foundation Ball. It was so important to Dominic and the Lodge that the event be a huge success. They needed some big donations to fund the next project they had planned. Of course, no one would know where the money would really be going. The only people who knew the exact nature of the project were the members of the Lodge.

"So what do you say, Ava? Will you take the contract?"

"Yes." She nodded her head, and he wondered if she needed to convince herself more than him. "Yes, I will."

"Great. I've got contracts here for you to sign."

"That confident, were you?"

"I like to have every base covered. If you'd said no then I wouldn't have mentioned them."

He passed the papers to Ava and gave her his pen. After she signed them, he countersigned and handed her back a copy. Satisfaction filled him that the first part of his plan had fallen into place.

Now to work on the next part of his plan. Cole had no doubt she would object strongly to it. Maybe he should take her to lunch to soften the blow.

"Do you want to go to lunch? Celebrate our new partnership?" he asked.

He could see the indecision cross her face and it cut him deep. He didn't like to see her debating with herself to have lunch with him. They were husband and wife. He'd treated her like a queen. Ava had been the one who had given up when things hadn't worked out the way she'd wanted. He should be the one wary about spending time with her. "Come on, Ava. Surely you're not afraid to spend time with me?"

As he suspected it would, her features cleared and determination replaced the indecision. "Of course I'm not. Lunch will be fine. After we're done I'll come back and collect all the information you have. I would like to get on the road before traffic gets crazy."

Cole made a noncommittal sound. He had no plans to let her go back to Margaret River. His name meant *Victory of the people* and he would be the victor in this battle. He'd already arranged for his caretaker's wife to pack up Ava's clothes and send them to his house. He knew she wasn't going to be happy with that.

"Let's go then," he said as he grabbed her hand and helped her to stand. The action brought her close to him. His body immediately hardened. Instinct took over and he pulled her closer while lowering his head to take possession of her lips. He sipped slowly at them. Savoring the feel of Ava back in his arms. Ava resisted for a moment before her body completely relaxed into his hold and her mouth opened beneath his. His hand trailed up, his fingers tangling in her hair, cupping her scalp, the temptation to lower her to the couch and lie over her, strong. Instead he pulled away, knowing that while his body may find release within Ava's warm depths, it wouldn't help his cause in getting Ava to live with him. He knew her well enough to know if she lost control in his arms, she'd regret it and want nothing more to do with him.

Placing a soft kiss on her nose, he took a step back, crossing his arms across his chest to stop the urge to forget his good intentions and pull her back into his embrace.

Silence descended around them, as if both had no idea what to say next. He wasn't usually speechless around women. With Ava he'd found that sometimes he didn't know what to say to her. On occasion she'd appeared unsure, as if any word he said he'd frighten her away. So he'd tried to show her what he wanted to say. Maybe he should've tried harder to talk.

"Are you ready for lunch?"

"What the hell are you playing at, Cole? Why did you kiss me?"

He wasn't going to say that once he had her in his arms again, he'd been so overcome with memories of the previous evening and their past relationship that he'd wanted to sample her again.

"Because you're my wife. And I wanted to."

He almost smiled as her mouth opened and closed a couple of times. His words had shocked himself as much as they had her. His plan hadn't been to tell her he'd wanted to taste her again.

"Cole, I—" she looked at the contract still in her hand and then back up at him. "—Don't think working with you is a good idea."

"It's a little too late for you to want to back out now, Ava. You're holding a legal and binding document in your hands. Walking away right now will be a breach of the contract we just signed. I'm sure you don't want to spend your hard earned money on a court battle."

"Are you serious?"

"Yes, I am. I don't have to time to play around with empty threats. This event is too important to all of us. I know you're the perfect person to help us make it a success. I want you on this job, Ava. Now, there will be no more talk of you walking away." Cole took her hand, ignoring the warmth her flesh against his generated. "Let's go to lunch."

Torture.

That's the only word Ava could use to describe sitting at a small table opposite Cole. Every time she went to move her legs they brushed up against his, causing darts of electricity to surge through her blood. Cole seemed totally unaffected by her touch. It only infuriated her even more. How he could be so impervious to her after the kiss they'd shared in his office? A kiss he'd initiated.

She focused back on the menu, pushing the memory of being back in Cole's arms as far away as possible.

"I didn't realize the menu was such an interesting read."

Ava flicked the laminated sheet down. "Better to read the menu than talk to you."

His sigh reached across table to her. She knew she sounded bitchy and childish but she wanted to dent his cool veneer.

"I'm sorry, that was uncalled for." She said. "It's just, this trip isn't turning out the way I thought it would."

The waiter arrived at that moment to take their orders, preventing Cole from responding to her. She asked for the pasta special and then handed the menu back to the waiter. Once he left, she braced herself to see what Cole was going to say next.

"So tell me, Ava, how did you see this trip turning out?"

A hint of steel underlined his casual tone. What did she tell him? That she thought he'd jump at the chance to divorce her? That's what she'd expected. His flat out *no* had surprised the hell out of her.

"Well, I didn't expect a job offer."

"No, I'm sure you didn't. I'm guessing," he paused as he took a swallow of his beer. "You thought I'd agree to your request for a divorce."

Taking a deep breath she voiced her innermost thoughts. "Yes I did. It makes sense, don't you think?"

"Why would divorcing make sense?"

"Because we never should've got married in the first place. Besides, we haven't been living together, like a normal married couple, for months."

"And whose fault is that? It's certainly not mine."

"Pettiness doesn't suit you, Cole. It doesn't matter what happens here in the restaurant. Once we're done here, I'll be getting back in my car and driving back home with everything I need to know about this job."

"You think it's going to be that easy? That I'm going to let you go back to the place where you won't answer my calls or my emails? That's not happening, Ava. The only place you're going after here is back to the office with me and then back to the home we shared."

"You cannot be serious."

He inclined his head briefly in response.

Fury like nothing she'd ever felt before rose up inside of her. The ruthless businessman had come out to play. She'd heard plenty about this side of Cole before they'd been married. His business acumen was widely known around business circles. He'd not only taken over the reins of the family company and made it more profitable, but he'd also accumulated his own wealth. He'd never been anything but gentle with her. She wasn't sure she liked seeing this ruthless side of him. She had to believe, even though he was being ruthless now, he'd keep his word and at the end of the job he'd agree to a divorce.

Their meals arrived at that moment so she waited until the server had placed their food in front of them and left before continuing. Although her meal looked delicious, the thought of eating didn't appeal.

She leaned forward. "Care to explain your last comment, about me living with you again?"

"It's simple really. I need to have you nearby. Due to the fact that we only have a few weeks until the event, you and I will be working together on this project. You living in Margaret River is not an option if we are to accomplish the work that needs to be completed."

While what he said made sense, the thought of cohabiting with Cole for any length of time wasn't a road she wanted to travel down again. The only reason she'd stayed away so long was because she knew if she continued to live with him, she'd fall further in love with him. Which would only lead to more heartache. Being in a one-sided relationship wasn't how she'd imagined her life going. An even scarier thought, what if she did go back to Cole and she ended up pregnant again? Then Cole would be tied to her forever. While a piece of her liked knowing she would always have a part of Cole, the other, more sensible piece told her that it would be an impossible situation to bear.

Ava gazed across the table at her estranged husband. His jaw set in a grim line of determination. Nothing she said would change his mind about her living with him.

"It seems I have no choice but to agree with this living arrangement. But I'll need to go back home to get my things. Close up the house."

"No need. I've arranged for the caretaker to come in and pack your clothes and ensure that the house is sorted. Besides, there is still a wardrobe full of your clothes at the house."

Ava cut into her food to avoid commenting on what Cole had just told her. Why had he kept her clothes? He'd said last night that being married *suited* him. How? In what way? And why did it suit him?

But then he'd agreed to a divorce this morning. He was sending out mixed signals and she wasn't sure she liked what he was doing. There would be only one way to find out.

She swallowed her food and took a sip of her water to moisten her throat. "Tell me something, Cole. You're sitting here telling me that I have to live with you. That we will be working closely together. That you still have a wardrobe full of my clothes. While also saying you'll give me a quick divorce at the end of the contract. So what exactly do you want?"

Silence surrounded them, the noise of the restaurant fading out, her attention totally on Cole and what he was going to say next. As the silence lengthened, Ava started to wonder if he would even answer her.

"What I want is for the event to be successful and having you close by is going to attain that. *If* you still want a divorce when the event is over, then I'll give it to you."

It sounded like he didn't want to divorce her at all. It didn't make any sense. He'd been such a player before they got together. He'd married her out of obligation. Oh, he'd never told her she or their child were obligations. But he also hadn't told her he loved her. She'd stopped telling him she loved him when she'd got out of hospital. Her grief had been all consuming and it had been easier to shut herself away. Succumb to the depression where she felt safe.

In her mind the reason they'd married was gone. She'd never felt more alone. Leaning on Cole wasn't an option. To use his strength to gain her own back—not an option.

On occasion, Ava had thought she'd seen pain in Cole's eyes when he'd tried to help her. But it passed so quickly she told herself she'd imagined those looks.

Watching him now, his features impassive and unreadable, she still wanted to reach out and touch his face. Trace the shape of his strong jaw; enjoy the scrape against her fingertips as she ran them over his lightly stubbled chin. Her body heated at the thought. Because she knew touching with her fingers would not be enough. She'd have to follow the path with her lips until she'd found his and lose herself in his kiss, like she had earlier in his office.

This was why she'd stayed away from Cole for as long as she had.

"Are my terms agreeable to you or not?"

Cole's words penetrated the thoughts she'd been lost in. Ava really didn't have much choice in the matter. If she wanted her freedom she was going to have to live with him. Work with him. Most important of all, try to resist him.

"Yes, Cole. I agree."

As a slow smile broke out over Cole's face, Ava wondered if she'd just made a deal with the devil.

CHAPTER 5

As Ava followed Cole's car up the windy driveway to the house, trepidation multiplied tenfold in her stomach. How was she ever going to be able to live under the same roof as Cole and not fall back into his arms? She had to be strong. She had to push him away. It was the only way she could survive the next few weeks.

She had to remember at the end of it all she would be a free woman and she would be able to move on with her life. Perhaps even find love again. The thought of giving her heart to someone who wasn't Cole didn't sit well with her. When she'd fallen in love with Cole she'd imagined it would be forever. That they would sit in the family room of their house at Christmas time with their children and their grandchildren surrounding them. That's how strong her love for Cole was.

No. No!

She was over him. She couldn't still think in terms of being in love with Cole.

Ava pulled her car to a stop and took a couple of deep breaths before opening her door. As she stepped out, she looked up and saw Cole standing beside her. A small smile playing around his lips.

"Welcome home."

"It hasn't been my home for a while now."

Cole looked like he was going to argue the point but she held up her hand to stop him. "Let's not go down this road again."

She brushed passed him and made her way up the stairs to the front door, hating that she had to wait for Cole to catch her up to her and unlock the door. As the big glass and wrought-iron door swung open, a thousand memories hit her one after the other. The most powerful being Cole carrying her down the stairs as her stomach twisted up on itself. The feeling of warm blood trickling down her leg. Her heart breaking with every second that passed, knowing exactly what the symptoms heralded.

Her feet wouldn't move. Her brain told them to move. To walk into the house but they weren't cooperating. Her legs had turned to stone.

Ava jumped when hands landed on her shoulder. The heat from their touch seeped into her, warming places that had frozen with the opening of the door.

"Talk to me, sweetheart. Tell me what's going on inside of you? I know something is."

She shook her head, trying to dispel the memories. "I was just remembering that awful day."

Cole enveloped her in a hug and maneuvered her across the threshold and into the magnificent foyer. The door slammed behind her and she looked up into Cole's eyes; pain and regret shone in their brown depths.

"I wish I could change that day. I wish I could wipe away the pain I see in your eyes." He paused and brushed a thumb against her cheek before stepping away. "I wish things could've been so different."

Finding courage deep inside, she brushed past Cole. "I wish things were different too."

Ava marched down the hallway toward the kitchen. She had no idea what she was going to do there. She needed breathing space from Cole. How could she think he felt the same way about her as she did about him? She'd told herself over and over she needed to break away from him. Now she found herself back in the house where she'd always felt like a visitor and never a rightful member. The first time she'd walked in she'd been starry-eyed with love, imagining this would be her home forever.

She opened the fridge door and stared at the contents, not really seeing what sat on the shelves.

"Found what you're looking for?"

She glanced over her shoulder and spied Cole leaning casually against the doorframe, arms crossed. He'd taken his jacket off and had loosened his tie. Instantly a memory hit of her meeting him as he opened the front door. Greeting him with a kiss and helping divest him of his jacket. Before she knew it, Cole had her up against the wall, taking her to heaven. Their relationship in the bedroom had never been an issue. Her body shivered. She knew it wasn't from the cool air emanating from the fridge.

Turning away from Cole, Ava opened the crisper drawer and plucked out a peach. She took a bite and juice trickled down her chin. She licked it up quickly.

It seemed so ridiculous to be standing in the kitchen. Neither one of them were speaking to each other.

"Did you want something, Cole?"

He pulled away from the doorframe and walked further into the kitchen. "I wanted to let you know that I'll be out this evening. I've got a Lodge rehearsal to go to."

Fantastic, her first night back and he's going to leave her alone. Why had he demanded she even stay at the house then? She could've gone back to her house and packed up, then returned to the office sometime tomorrow morning. She didn't understand Cole's actions or his need to have her return to their marital home.

Not that she had a problem where he was going, just that he was leaving her alone. When they'd been together she'd never questioned his involvement with the Freemasons. Her knowledge extended to Cole attending rehearsals and then a week later attending the actual formal meetings.

During the time they'd been living apart, whenever she'd wanted to try and feel close to him she'd googled Freemasons. There were pages of links. In the end she hadn't read any of the articles she'd clicked on. She'd convinced herself that no knowledge was better for her and her attempts to purge Cole from her life.

Now, having some distance between them, she could finally admit the secrecy of what happened when he went to his meetings bothered her. She knew for a fact that one of the Lodges he attended was right next door to a gentleman's club. Did he really go to a meeting or was he being "entertained" by other women?

Ava had heard plenty of joking about some of their activities. For so many years an aura of secrecy shrouded them. Even now, with all the information available on the internet, people still speculated on what happened behind closed doors at Freemason meetings.

"What do you have to rehearse, riding the billy goat? Or maybe you have to make sure you've got the altar set up correctly to sacrifice the virgin." She couldn't help lashing out at Cole for making her come back and live with him, and then leaving her alone the first night she was back in the house.

"Yes, it's important we get the angle right on the cuts we make on the sacrificial virgin. And," he deadpanned her. "It takes a lot of practice to ride the billy goat."

"You'd think after all this time you wouldn't need to *rehearse*."

Ava stood her ground as Cole stalked closer to her. A muscle ticked in his jaw. This was the first time she'd deliberately provoked him into an argument.

"What is it you're trying to say?"

"Nothing."

"Really?" He stood right in front of her. He crossed his arms over his chest and widened his stance. "If you want to say something, just say it, instead of the wise-ass cracks about Freemasonry."

"Why ask me to come here today when you knew you were going out tonight? Why couldn't I have gone back to my house, packed everything up and then come back in a couple of days? Now

I'm going to be stuck *here*, by myself, while you go off doing your thing."

"*Your* house is really *my* house and you know why you're here. It's just unfortunate that I have to be out tonight."

"You're an asshole, do you know that?"

Ava went to brush past him but his arm shot out, wrapping around her waist, halting her exit from the kitchen. "And you weren't being a bitch with your comments?"

Ava supposed she deserved him snapping back at her. She couldn't deny the label hurt her. Just like calling him an asshole probably hurt him.

She closed her eyes. What were they doing to each other?

As if he'd he could read her thoughts, Cole's grip on her softened and he pulled her closer to him. He put his other arm around her to secure her against him.

"I'm sorry, sweetheart. I don't want to fight with you." His lips brushed the top her hair.

Being so close to him. Being kissed on the top of her head. Being held in his arms messed with her resolve to keep her distance and remain immune to him. What she did know was that she didn't want to fight with him either. To get through the time until after the gala event, having a friendly relationship with Cole was the most important thing. It didn't matter what he did with the Lodge. Once she had her divorce she would never have to worry about Cole or his Freemason cronies.

But she needed to reduce the amount of physical contact they shared. She pushed gently against his chest. "I don't want to fight either."

Ava breathed easier when Cole released his hold on her and put some distance between them. "I'm sorry I have to go out tonight, Ava, but it's important that I go."

"I know," she sighed as she bit into her peach again.

"Why don't you order a pizza for dinner while I go shower and change?"

Ava nodded and immediately walked over to the drawer where they'd kept the takeout menus when they'd lived together before. As she opened it, she felt a semblance of relief pour over her that some things hadn't changed since she'd moved out.

"Are there any particular toppings you want?"

"I don't have a preference. Order whatever you'd like." Cole said as he started to unbutton his shirt.

Ava studied the menu intently so she wouldn't be tempted to stare as he revealed his hard chest to her. A chest she remembered laying her head on and feeling so loved.

Would she ever feel that type of love again?

CHAPTER 6

Cole tapped his pen on his notepad. His mind wasn't on the meeting, but on Ava. He hated having to leave her home on her first night back with him. But he needed to be at this meeting. The Lodge rehearsal was over and now he was with Dominic, Jude and Declan discussing the next step in their plans. He should be paying attention. The gala was an important event and they needed to make sure they had the right people attending. They couldn't let a whiff of what they were really doing get out amongst the public. If it did, all their hard work would be for nothing.

"Cole? Did you hear what I said?" Dominic's voice broke through his thoughts.

"Sorry, what did you say?"

Dominic sat back and mirrored Cole's action of tapping his pen on the table. "Why don't you tell me what's really going on. You've been distracted all evening. Which is so unlike you. Is it Ava?"

He should've realized he couldn't keep much away from Dominic. He was far too observant. It also meant that if he tried to say everything was fine, Dominic wouldn't believe him.

"Yes, it's Ava."

"You need to cut her loose, man." Jude drawled out. "She's not worth losing sleep over."

In a flash Cole was standing as the red mist of anger enveloped him. He leaned over the small table, grabbing Jude's shirt and getting in his face. "That's my wife you're talking about. She's worth more than the women you hang out with. Don't you *ever* say she's not worth anything."

A hand clamped on his shoulder and Cole released his hold on Jude, shocked at his actions. Jude was one of his good friends. Sure he was a player, like he used to be, but ultimately Jude didn't deserve to be treated that way.

"Are you okay?" Declan asked quietly. Always the protector of the group. The one who kept the peace.

Cole scrubbed a hand down his face. He owed his friend an apology. "Yeah, I'm fine." He held out his hand toward Jude. "Sorry, man. I didn't mean to go off at you like that."

Jude took his hand and gave it a slight squeeze. "No worries. I'm sorry too; I shouldn't have said what I did."

"Right, now that that's settled, can we get back to business?" asked Dominic.

Everyone around the room nodded and Cole sat back down. He couldn't believe he'd let his emotions get the better of him like that. Jude was one of his best friends. The four of them in the room had been friends for years. Dominic, Jude and Declan had been there for him when his father had died. They'd got drunk with him after his father's funeral. They'd been there when Ava hadn't.

"I'll leave the subject of what you and Ava are doing, but I want to know if she's on board for the gala? We have to get these invitations out and final preparations started."

Taking a deep breath and pushing thoughts of Ava alone in the house aside, Cole answered. "Yes, she is. She signed a contract this morning. I gave her everything the previous planner had prepared." He laughed ruefully as he remembered her response to seeing what concept the other planner had come up with. "I can safely say that she was as unimpressed as we were with the previous concepts. We'll be working on it more tomorrow."

Dominic raised an eyebrow. "Are you going to be comfortable working so closely with her?"

Was he? Yes he was. There was so much more at stake than coming up with gala invitations.

"Yes. It'll be fine." He met Dominic's gaze, letting his friend know he had nothing to be concerned about. "This project is too important to let my personal feelings cloud what we're trying to achieve."

As if seeing something within Cole that assuaged his concerns, Dominic nodded and looked back at his notes.

"Right, let's get back to things. I received an email from the contact we have in Malaysia. He said that a cargo ship left Port Kelang two days ago and it's slated to arrive in Fremantle in eleven days. The ships are usually here for five days, but this one is getting some maintenance work done on it so it will be here for two weeks. You know what that means, don't you?"

"Yes, they're going to be able to get twice as many kids as they normally do," said Jude, as he curled his fingers into fists.

"How many have we got in the homes?" asked Cole.

"We're almost at capacity but we have room for about twenty more." Dominic picked up a folder and flicked through the contents.

"According to Sienna there are about seven girls and eight boys who've completed their two years of working and attending classes. They have found stable jobs and have enough money to get a place of their own. She said they probably will be moving out within the next month or two."

"That means there could be an overlap," mused Declan.

"Yes, which is why it's important we try and raise more funds than first projected to see if we can buy another apartment complex to house more kids. Not to mention to have enough money to pay the special ops team." Dominic paused and looked at Jude. "How soon before the team gets back?"

"They should be back next week. Hopefully with more information about some of the locations where the kids are in Malaysia who need to be brought back home."

As Jude clenched his jaw, Cole knew Jude was hoping that the next lot of information they received would have news on his sister, Renee, who'd gone missing two years ago. It was her disappearance and the speculation that she'd been sold into sex slavery that started this whole side venture of theirs. No one was able to get information like Freemasons. With a worldwide organization, the fraternity of brotherhood was strong. A mason always helped out a fellow mason. The secrecy they were known for allowed them to do more than surface charity works. The charity the gala raised money for was just the tip of the iceberg.

To the general public, Lodge Drysor raised money to fund accommodations for homeless teenagers. Giving the street kids the opportunity to get clean if they'd traveled down the road of drug use. Or a warm bed and food in their belly if they had no other place to go. Once clean, they would then take classes to finish their education and learn to be savvy with money. Part of the agreement for the kids to live in the accommodation was they needed to get a job.

Dominic had wanted to ensure the kids had job opportunities. He'd proposed the idea of purchasing a couple of established fast food restaurants for the kids to work in. They'd all agreed it was a wonderful idea and had used their own personal funds to make the purchase. Another idea of Dominic's had been to employ the odd homeless adult. Give them an opportunity to start their lives over again. Help them feel worthwhile again. Some even got their families back. It was rewarding and he was honored to be part of an organization like Freemasonry that had people, like Dominic, whose focus was to help the community.

It also proved to be a salvation for the girls and boys who had been plucked off the streets and taken away from their families. Taken to places where they experienced things no young person should ever experience in their life. At the shelter they were able to receive the counseling they needed before being returned to their families. Or, if they had no families, getting a place of their own.

Cole had never imagined following his father's footsteps into Freemasonry would forge deep friendships and create so many things for the community. Do so much more than he'd ever imagined.

But it came at a price. It was important that not all of their endeavors became public knowledge. The risk was too great. One slip of the tongue could hurt too many people.

Keeping information from Ava didn't sit well with him. He knew, though, that his allegiance was to the brotherhood of the Freemasons—no matter the cost to his personal life. Besides, when they'd been together she never seemed bothered when he didn't say too much about what happened at his meetings.

Until tonight, when she'd made her smart comments when he'd told her he was going out.

"So what's the plan going to be?" Cole asked Dominic.

"We haven't worked everything out as yet. Our priority is to make sure the gala is in order before we can think about how we're going to handle the ship when it comes into port, so that when it leaves it won't have any innocent kids on board."

"Agreed," they all said in unison.

Cole closed the door from the garage into the kitchen quietly. He smiled when he noticed that the kitchen light had been left on. For the past few months the house had always been cloaked in darkness when he returned home. He flicked the light off and headed toward the stairs, noting another light shining at the top of the landing. Ava leading the way to her; only she wasn't, not really.

At the bottom of the stairs he paused. He hoped when he walked up the stairs and entered his room, he'd see the outline of Ava in his bed. He knew the likelihood of that happening was nil.

He climbed the staircase, and instead of going to the right he turned left and headed down the hallway. He hadn't been down this part of the house since Ava walked out on him. He hadn't wanted to admit that she had gone so he'd avoided the room where she'd spent the three months after their wedding.

As he approached the room he heard the muted sound of voices. It took him a moment to realize Ava had the television on. It seemed strange for her to be up so late. He'd left Dominic and the others after midnight.

"Ava?" He knocked quietly on the door. There was no answer so he opened the door and saw Ava curled on her side, facing the door, sound asleep. She looked so peaceful. He was about to step out of the room when he thought he should turn the television off. When he reached the cabinet he noticed something sparkling in the glow of the television. He reached and picked up the earrings. Cole brushed his thumb over the gems. In his hand he held the earrings he had given to Ava as a wedding present.

A small smile crept over his face as he recalled the wide grin on her face as she walked down the aisle toward him at their wedding. Her hair had been put into an intricate design atop of her head. His wedding gift of earrings glittered in the sunlight. The drop emerald earrings kissed her neck as they swayed with each step she took. She'd never looked more beautiful.

Cole hadn't noticed her wearing them today but he had noticed them the night of his mother's charity event. He was surprised she still had them. The last time he'd seen them she had been throwing them at him as they'd argued about god knows what now. They'd argued about stupid things. He'd walked out of the room and she'd walked out of the house and hadn't returned until today.

Clutching the earrings for a few more seconds, he placed them on the cabinet and turned the television off. Immediately the room darkened.

What would Ava think if he slipped in beside her? If he gathered her close and held her, like he'd wanted to when she'd been hurting so badly six months ago.

He moved slowly toward the bed, halting when he reached the side where Ava lay. Her brow furrowed, as if she was having a bad dream. His hand moved and brushed a thumb across her warm skin, smoothing out the lines.

Giving into the urge to be close to her, Cole leaned down and pressed his lips softly against hers.

It was the briefest of touches but his blood fired to life. If he wasn't careful he'd find himself following through on his earlier thought of joining her in the bed.

He went to pull away but stopped when a hand landed on his cheek.

"Cole? Is that really you?" Ava whispered the words into the darkness.

Cole placed his hand over hers. "Yes, sweetheart, it's me."

"You came. I didn't think you would."

Something about the way she spoke stilled the rapid beating of his heart. Was she talking about now, or had she been hoping he'd come down to the country house and see her? There were many times he'd got into the car to go down and see her, but had stopped at the last minute. Remembering how she'd told him she hadn't wanted to see him ever again. That he'd ruined her life.

He also wondered if she was dreaming. He leaned down and noticed her eyes were still shut. Knowing he couldn't take advantage of her, he removed her hand from where it still lay against his cheek and placed it on the sheets.

"Sleep, sweetheart, I'll be here in the morning." He placed another kiss on her lips and walked out of the room. Not looking back, knowing if he did he'd forget all his good intentions and gather her close and spend the rest of the night holding her tightly.

CHAPTER 7

An incessant buzzing penetrated the fog of sleep engulfing Ava. When had her alarm buzzed so loudly? Usually she woke to the laughing voices of the breakfast crew from her favorite radio station. She reached over and found air. Something wasn't right. She opened her eyes and stared at the ceiling. Realization struck. She wasn't at her house. She was back in Cole's house. Back in the room she'd moved into after her miscarriage.

She groaned and closed her eyes again, wanting sleep to take her back but knowing she needed to get up. The reason she was back in this house was because she had a job to do. A job working with Cole.

Throwing back the covers, she reached across the bed and slammed her hand down on the alarm clock, ending the annoying sound it was making.

She was padding toward the bathroom when she stopped and looked at the television. It was off. She was pretty sure she'd fallen asleep with it on. She'd found that that was the only way she could fall asleep after she'd moved down to Margaret River.

Had she turned it off because she knew she wasn't alone in the house?

A memory teased the corners of her mind. Cole lips on hers. Her hand on his cheek. She had been positive she'd been dreaming. Had it been real? Had he been in her room last night?

She remembered she hadn't wanted him to leave her alone in bed. But she couldn't form the words to stop him from leaving.

"This is pointless," she muttered out loud. It wasn't that big of a deal if he came into her room.

Pushing the memory of Cole and his touch out of her mind, she headed for the shower. Hoping it would clear her mind so she could face the day without letting on how much she'd wanted Cole to join her in bed.

Ava walked into the kitchen, relieved to see that Cole hadn't made his way downstairs. It surprised her because he always rose early. She reached into the fridge to pull out some juice when she heard the door from the garage open.

She closed the fridge and her greeting to Cole died in her throat. He hadn't noticed her standing in the room. He was wiping his face with the tank top he'd just removed. His abs rippled with the movement. His jogging shorts hugged his legs, showcasing his muscles.

"Morning." The word squeaked out of her and she cleared her throat. "I forgot you ran."

Unable to say anything else, she watched mesmerized as he lowered the top from his face. He glanced at his watch. "Why are you up so early?"

"It's not early, if anything you're going to be late if you don't get a move on."

Cole walked over to her and she gripped the juice she was holding a little tighter.

"I'm right on time, it's only six o'clock."

"What? I set my alarm for six, which was over half an hour ago."

Cole pointed to the clock on the wall. "I think your clock must be wrong."

Ava checked, and sure enough she had got up early. "Well, I guess that means I'll get a head start to my day."

What she really wanted to do was sidle up to Cole and run her hands over his chest. He looked so strong and she'd ached for so long to be held by him again.

"I'm going to take a shower, but we can leave as soon as I get back so we can both get a head start on the day."

Ava could only nod. Her mind immediately went to Cole naked beneath the water. She jumped when he kissed her briefly on the cheek before he disappeared out of the kitchen.

She stumbled over to the stools sitting at the island counter and pulled one out to sit on. She closed her eyes and took some deep breaths. Already, after a single day, all she wanted to do was lose herself in Cole's arms again.

For goodness sake, the man hadn't ever told her loved her. Why would she even think he'd want to rekindle their relationship? Sure, he'd kissed her like there was no tomorrow. That was simply sexual attraction. They'd always been in sync when it came to that part of their relationship. It was the sharing feelings part where they'd completely failed. So many times she wished they could have a do-over. A second chance to say or do things so they could do it right.

Opening her eyes, she glanced around the kitchen. Nothing had changed, but she felt like she'd changed. Had they been given a second chance? Was it possible? Did she even want to try and have a second chance with Cole? Did he?

The juice was still grasped in her hand so she put it on the counter. Her stomach swirled so much with indecision, she knew if she ate or drank anything it would sit like a lead balloon in her stomach.

A sound had her turning her head and she saw Cole standing in the kitchen doorway. Her mouth dried. He was wearing a dark grey suit and white shirt. A lavender-colored tie hung loosely around his neck, ready to be tied in preparation for the day. Her fingers itched to pick up the fabric and tie the knot. It wasn't the first time she'd tied his tie for him. It had always ended with a steamy kiss and sometimes a trip back to the bedroom.

Ruthlessly, she pushed those thoughts away. She wasn't going back there with Cole. She couldn't. She had to get through the next few weeks and then their relationship would be done. If she let the feelings she knew she still had for Cole come to the forefront of her mind, recovering from their inevitable break up would be something she wasn't sure she could ever get over. Nothing good came from a one-sided love affair and that was what they had. She had to remember that the only reason they'd even got married was because she had been pregnant at the time. Ava wasn't Cole's usual girl. She represented a step out of the box for him. Someone who had ended up pregnant and he'd done the noble thing in marrying her. She'd told him he didn't have to but he'd insisted.

Then the night after their wedding, when they'd returned to the house before they were to leave on their honeymoon, she'd lost the baby.

"Ava?" A hand touched her cheek, chasing away the thoughts rioting through her mind.

She looked up into Cole's eyes, noting the concern shining in their depths. At his sharp intake of breath she lowered her eyes, knowing the shadow of pain from her dark thoughts still had to be lurking in her own eyes.

Cole let out a curse before he closed the gap between them and his lips brushed gently against hers. As his hands framed her face, her resistance to him cracked a little more. Her hands crept under his jacket and up the strong muscles of his back. As his lips encouraged hers to open, she responded, allowing their tongues to touch gently before retreating.

Slowly he surrendered his hold on her face, and smoothed a hand over her hair as his lips pulled away from hers. He rested his forehead against hers, their ragged breathing the only sound in the room.

Summoning up courage from deep within, Ava took first one step, then another and another, until about four feet stood between them. Her fingers touched her lips, still warm from Cole's kiss.

"We have to stop doing that," she murmured.

"Why?"

"Because kissing will only confuse the situation between us. We're getting a divorce, Cole. I shouldn't be here. I should move into a hotel or something."

"No." The word fired out of him and his hands paused in the motion of doing up his tie. "You are staying here and there will be no talk of you moving out. Now let's go so we don't get caught in morning rush hour."

His violent dismissal of her idea of moving out surprised her. She'd never taken Cole as being domineering. He'd never forced her into uncomfortable situations, but this time he had.

"Why shouldn't I go to a hotel?"

Cole had finished knotting his tie and strode over to her. "Let me repeat myself, Ava. This time perhaps it would be wise for you to listen. You. Are. Not. Moving. Out. Now, the subject is closed."

She opened her mouth to argue but Cole held up his hand. "Do you want me to kiss you again, Ava? Because let me tell you, that will be no hardship at all."

Everything about the way he held himself told Ava that arguing with him would be useless.

"Yes."

His eyebrow rose at her response and she had to quickly run through what they'd been talking about prior to her answer.

Kissing. He said did she want him to kiss her again.

"I mean no," she quickly blurted out. Taking a deep breath, counting to five before exhaling, she continued. "What I mean is, yes, I understand that I'm staying here and, no, I don't want you to kiss me again."

A lazy grin broke out over Cole's face. "I believe one part of your answer. The second part I'm not so sure about."

Ava rolled her eyes in frustration at his innuendos. "Can we just leave now, please?"

"Sure." He looked around the kitchen as if searching for something. "Do you have everything?"

For a second she wondered what Cole could be talking about, then realization struck. "Give me five minutes while I grab my handbag and laptop. I'll meet you in the car."

With quick movements, she brushed passed Cole and headed back toward her room. One of the first things she planned to do would be to let Cole know that after today, she would find her own way to the office. She had her car. She could be independent. There was no reason at all for them to have to spend time going to and from work together. She needed her space and driving would give her that. Only knowing Cole, if she mentioned driving herself, he would fight her on that matter as well.

Ava had a feeling Cole had plans to spend as much time with her as possible. Somehow she had to work out a way to keep herself from falling under his spell again.

CHAPTER 8

The letters in the email coalesced into a jumble Cole couldn't decipher. He swiveled his chair away from his desk and looked out the window. The drive into the office had been quiet; neither he nor Ava had felt the need to talk. He'd spent the drive coming to terms with seeing so much pain in Ava's eyes. He had seen the same desolate look when the doctor had confirmed Ava had miscarried their baby. She had been inconsolable. For the first time in his life, Cole had felt completely useless. He couldn't fix what had happened. He couldn't bring the baby back. He couldn't trade places with Ava and take the pain away from her.

Was it any wonder she'd closed down? He hadn't been able to express what he had been experiencing, seeing her doubled over in pain. He closed his eyes but the memory of blood trickling down her leg couldn't be erased.

"Cole, have you got a minute?"

He whirled his chair around and saw the object of his thoughts standing in the doorway. She held a pile of different colored paper and had her iPad tucked under her arm.

He got up and strode over to where she stood, relieving her of the paper. "Sure, have a seat." He indicated the couches. "Do you want some coffee? I can get Fiona to arrange it."

"No, I'm fine. I haven't drunk coffee for a while now."

Cole took a seat on the couch opposite Ava, cognizant of the fact they were sitting the exact same way as they had been yesterday.

"Fiona can get you anything you want."

She looked up from where she had been studying something on her iPad. "I'm fine, Cole."

"Okay. So what can I help you with?"

"I've done some mock-ups of a new invitation. I know that you weren't happy with what the previous designer came up with. Although I didn't mind the idea of using trees and lights as a symbolic nod to the charity's name."

She spoke with authority and confidence. Having never worked with Ava before or seen her in a corporate environment, Cole had to admit he found this version of Ava very alluring. He had to adjust his trousers. Although that wasn't anything new when it came to his body's reaction to Ava.

"Cole, are you listening?"

Pulling his thoughts back to the task at hand. "Sorry. What were you saying? Something about still incorporating trees and lights?"

"Good to know you were paying attention."

"Is that sarcasm I hear?"

Ava laughed. "No, just dry derision."

Cole couldn't help himself, he reached across the small gap and placed a hand on her cheek. "I like hearing you laugh."

And just like that the atmosphere changed. Her skin so smooth and soft beneath his fingers. He trailed his fingertips over her cheek, pushing a strand of hair off her face.

"Cole?" she whispered, as her hand came up and landed on his.

They sat there for endless moments. Looking at each other. Hands touching softly. When her tongue darted out to moisten her lips, it took everything in him to not pull her toward him so he could sample her. Lose himself in the essence that was Ava.

Instead he smiled and pulled his hand out from under hers. As much as he wanted to bury himself deep within her, he knew they had an awful lot to sort out. He wanted her back. Wanted Ava living with him full time. He wanted their marriage to work. He knew, instinctively, that he needed to show Ava he didn't just want her body. He wanted her mind and her soul. He wanted the whole package.

Cole stood and cleared his throat. He walked over to the cabinet sitting beside the couches and opened the small fridge. He pulled out two bottles of water. Regardless of what Ava said, he needed something to cool himself down.

"I don't know about you, but I need this." He held out one of the bottles toward her. Their fingers brushing when she took it from him.

Cole wrenched the lid of his bottle and took a couple of long swallows, hoping the cold water would cool down the heat building in him. When he felt he had himself better under control, he sat down again. Making sure to control any urges he had to touch Ava.

"So here's what I'm thinking." Ava turned around her iPad to show him the design. In the middle of the screen sat a tree that looked like arms entwined, lights on the branches. Engraved in the middle of the tree trunk was the square and compass—the universal sign of Freemasonry.

He studied it for a bit longer, trying to work out why it worked so well.

Oh god, he didn't like her mock-up. He thought it was as bad as the other invite. Damn, she didn't have any more time to rework another invite. Not with the tight timeline they were working with.

"Ava," Cole interrupted her internal rambling. "I love it. I think it's perfect. There's something about it that embraces everything we're trying to achieve with the charity. You've done a great job."

As her shoulders relaxed, Ava let out the breath she had been holding and allowed herself to bask in the smile Cole directed at her.

One hurdle passed, now onto the next one. Working out which paper to print the invites on. She had to get it to the printers by eleven o'clock. They told her they'd be able get them back to her by two o'clock.

"Next thing. I've spoken to the printer I always use and they've promised me they can do a rush job and get the invites printed up quickly so we can get them distributed today."

"That's great. You've got everything under control."

When he went to stand, Ava held up her hand. "Not so fast, hotshot." The nickname she'd occasionally called him flowed off her tongue, like water flowing down a mountain.

He crossed his arms across his chest and quirked his eyebrow. "Yes?"

The glimmer of amusement in his eyes prevented her from snapping back at him. "I still need your input. Can you sit down again?"

"You have my undivided attention."

No one could be more dangerous than Cole when he set his mind to flirting with someone. He'd reeled her in that way when they'd first met. Not that she'd put up much of a fight. She'd known who Cole was. His reputation preceded him. The fact she held his interest had warmed her soul.

Stop.

She told herself she had a job to do and already things had almost got out of hand, when Cole had touched her cheek.

Focusing her attention back to the piles of paper in front of her, she selected some of her favorite pieces.

"We have to work out what color and type of paper or card you want the invites printed on."

Cole pointed to one. "The one that looks the best."

She rolled her eyes. "You know you should take the time to look at each piece and decide if it's what you want. Some of these options are pretty pricey. You need to make sure you're happy with your selections."

"We don't care. The caliber of people coming to the event warrant the best type of card the invite can be printed on."

Ava liked nothing better than to have an unlimited budget to work with. It made the process so much easier if the client wasn't penny-pinching on every aspect of the job. She shuffled through the assortment of paper and card she had already picked out and laid two on the table. Her initial thoughts had been to go with red but as she looked through, she decided that the thick cream card would be more suitable. That way she could play with the colors on the front of the invite to make them pop more. She chose a lighter weight cream rice paper as the inner page where the details of the party would be printed.

"What do you think of these two?"

Cole picked up both items, turning them in his hands. Ava bit her lip to stop herself from laughing as his brow furrowed in concentration, obviously taking her earlier advice to heart.

"You really have no idea what to look for, do you?" she blurted out, unable to stop the laughter from shooting out of her.

He shrugged his shoulders and grinned widely. "No I don't." He placed the papers back on the table. "Sweetheart, I trust your judgment. I trust that you will do the best thing for the gala, the charity and the Lodge."

Tears welled in her eyes. To have Cole's absolute faith and trust in her had been the last thing she'd been expecting when she'd walked into his office. She knew this job was extremely important to him and his friends. She planned to do her very best to make sure the event raised a lot of money.

"Thank you."

The urge to walk around to where he sat on the couch and kiss him on the lips bubbled up inside of her. She pushed the urge down. The safest thing for her, right now, would be to walk back to her office and get on the phone with the printer to finalize the invitations.

"Is there anything else you need me for at the moment?" Cole asked.

The layout of the dinner menu still needed to be sorted out, as well as place cards and other things. She also had some ideas about a signature cocktail and a chocolate fountain. But she held off asking Cole. Putting distance between the two of them seemed like a good idea again. Hopefully the information she needed to find out would be in the files that were still piled up on her desk.

Collecting her materials, she stood. "Nope, if I need anything else I'll let Fiona know that I need to speak with you."

"Ava, my door is always open for you. You don't need to check with Fiona if I'm free. You obviously didn't this time."

Warmth rose from the bottom of her neck, filling her cheeks. "Well, she wasn't at her desk, and when I looked in you appeared to be daydreaming."

"Daydreaming, huh? I'll have you know I don't daydream."

"Sure looked like it to me."

The phone ringing prevented any more banter between them. Cole strode over to his desk, but before he picked up the receiver he looked at her again. "Remember, any time, any place, my door is always open."

Giving him a slight nod, Ava walked out of the office, knowing he wasn't talking about his office door.

CHAPTER 9

"I'm leaving now, Cole. Do you need me for anything else?"

Cole looked up from the report he was reading. Fiona stood in the doorway, handbag in hand ready to leave for the day.

"No, I don't have anything that's urgent. Besides, I know it's Julian's birthday tomorrow and you probably have a cake to make. What does he want this year? Ninja Turtle?"

Fiona laughed as she took a couple of steps into his office. "I don't make the cake, that's one job Evan does. He's far better at it than me. If I had the job of making a cake, I'd go to the store and buy a sheet cake already decorated."

"Sounds far easier to do."

"Well, Evan enjoys doing it and his attention to detail is amazing. Julian wants a Deadpool cake this year."

"Deadpool? What's a *deadpool*?"

"It's a Marvel comic character. Not one of the good guys either. Although I think he turns good. Julian is very into his video games, like most ten-year-old boys."

"Sounds far too complicated to me." Cole waved his hand. "Go and have fun cake-making. Besides, it's Friday; you shouldn't be working late on a Friday night."

"Neither should you, boss. Shouldn't you be taking your wife home?"

"Yes, shouldn't you be doing that?" Another voice entered the conversation.

Cole shifted his attention from Fiona to Ava, standing leaning against the doorframe. She looked tired. A quick glance at the clock on his laptop told him it was after 6.30 p.m. After her early morning start, no wonder Ava looked like she could collapse on his couch and fall straight to sleep.

"Give me two minutes to shut down my computer and then we're out of here."

Ava nodded and Fiona murmured a goodbye. As he went through the motions of shutting everything down, he watched Ava. Leaning against the doorframe, stifling yet another yawn. She looked as beautiful now as she had this morning when he'd walked into the kitchen after his run.

"What do you want to do for dinner?" she asked as they made their way toward the elevators.

"Not sure. Do you want to stop at a restaurant on the way home?" he asked as he ushered Ava into the elevator and hit the button for the basement.

"Not really. I'd just rather go back home. Change into some comfy clothes and relax on the couch."

"How about we order some Chinese and watch a movie. I'll even let you pick a chick flick to watch?"

Ava stopped and looked up at him, skepticism etched in her green eyes. "Really? You'd watch a chick flick?"

They reached his car and he opened the door for her. "Yes, I'd watch a chick flick with you tonight." Cole put his briefcase on the ground and leaned forward, resting his cheek against hers. He whispered in her ear. "I'd do anything for you tonight, Ava."

He stepped back, expecting her to get into the car. Only she didn't. She stood as still as a statue.

"Are you getting in?"

He saw her jump and give herself a little shake. Wordlessly she slipped into the car.

Cole smiled as he softly shut the door. He liked getting Ava off balance.

The aroma of Chinese food greeted her as she walked into the kitchen. Cole was busy taking plastic containers out of plastic bag. He had on denim jeans that looked well-worn and hugged his ass nicely. The black t-shirt molded his chest. The fabric stretching across his biceps had her clenching her hands into fists to stop the urge to touch him.

She opened her mouth but nothing came out. She swallowed and tried again. "Looks like I timed it well."

Cole looked up and smiled. "Yep, perfect timing. Do you want chopsticks or a fork?"

Ava walked over to the kitchen island to see what food Cole had ordered. "I'll go for chopsticks."

"Why don't you grab the wine I've opened, and glasses, and take them into the media room. I'll dish up the food and bring it to you."

"I can get my own food, you know." Her words came out harsher than she intended.

Cole's face tightened. "I know that, but I want to do this for you. However, if you don't trust me," he stepped away from the counter and opened his arms wide. "Help yourself."

He picked up a plate and started filling it with food. Remorse immediately filled her. Why was she being such a bitch? Cole wanted to do something nice for her. Why couldn't she accept it?

Ava walked over to where Cole stood, attacking the fried rice as if it were an annoying fly. She placed her hand on his arm, stopping him from adding more to his plate. She reached up and turned his face toward hers. Ava wanted Cole looking at her when she said what she wanted to say. "I'm sorry, Cole. I don't know why I snapped at you. Thank you, I'd love for you to serve me dinner."

Time stood still as they looked into each other's eyes. For a few moments, Ava wondered if Cole would even respond to her.

Finally he nodded and smiled, except the smile didn't reach his eyes. She could kick herself for breaking his good mood. "Go. I'll be with you in a few minutes."

"Okay. Thanks, Cole."

He grunted a response and Ava went over to the counter and grabbed the bottle of merlot and glasses that Cole had set out for them.

Even though a tense atmosphere still surrounded them, Ava felt hopeful that once they'd eaten and had a couple of glasses of wine, the tension would disappear.

She walked into the media room and set the wine and glasses on the low, squat coffee table. Over to the left sat a built-in unit, which she knew housed the movies. Opening one of the drawers, she flicked through the choices.

Her fingers paused when she spied the plain gold case with the words "Our Wedding" in scroll print on the spine. They'd never sat down and watched the DVD of their wedding. They'd never been in the right place in their relationship to watch it. They still weren't.

"Have you found something to watch?"

"Uh, no, not yet. I'm trying to find something that we'll both enjoy."

Ava heard the sound of plates being placed on the table. The thick carpet muffled Cole's steps, but her body, so in tune with his, knew the moment he stepped up behind her.

A shiver rippled down her spine when his hands landed on her shoulders. His fingers started a slow massage on her tight muscles.

"Sweetheart, I'm serious," he murmured the words in her ear. "I'm happy to watch whatever you want."

Flustered by the sensation of Cole still massaging her shoulders and talking softly to her, she fumbled around the drawer and plucked out the first one she could get a grip on.

"How about this one?" Cole's hands immediately stilled. Ava looked at the DVD in her hand.

Whether it was her subconscious mind, or a wicked twist of fate, she found herself holding up their wedding video.

Clearing his throat Cole took a step back and Ava missed the touch of his hands on her. "I'm not sure that would be the best idea."

Ava stuffed it back in the drawer and closed it with a snap. "Maybe not. How about we just see what's on the television?"

She slipped past Cole and picked up a wine glass, taking a hefty sip. The wine burned slightly as it went down her throat. Placing the glass back on the table, she picked up the plate Cole had prepared and sat down on the couch, tucking her legs on the cushion next to her.

Silently, Cole sat next to her. He stretched his legs out so that they rested on the coffee table. The light spicy scent of his cologne wafted toward her. She sniffed appreciatively, glad that he hadn't changed his cologne since they'd been apart.

The sound of their chopsticks clacking against their plates was the only sound in the room. Ava wished Cole would turn the television on or say something to her. Maybe she should say something to him.

"How was the rest of your day?"

Cole finished his mouthful before answering. "Busy. How about yours? I didn't see you after you showed me the invites. I take it you were able to get them out on time?"

"Yep, everyone should be getting their invites on Monday and the RSVPs should start rolling in a few days after that. I did want to speak to you about how you wanted the tables set up and if you had a preference for who should sit with whom."

"I think Dominic's assistant has got some notes on that. Remind me to send him an email and he can make sure you get it by Monday.

"Okay, that sounds good."

Their conversation trailed off and Ava methodically lifted food to her mouth, chewed then swallowed. When she had cleared her plate, Cole took it from her and exited the room again.

Wanting to have some noise in the room, Ava grabbed the remote from the table and turned the television on, clicking through the channels, not really paying attention to the images flashing before her. Eventually the sound of laughter pulled her from her trance and she stopped. One of the channels had reruns of one of her favorite comedies. Placing the remote back on the table she sat back, hoping Cole would enjoy the show as well.

"Oh, this show is funny. I didn't know it was on tonight."

Cole sat down next to her and draped his arm across the back of the couch, his fingers resting on her shoulders.

The longer they sat together the more her body relaxed. Soon she forgot that she shouldn't be feeling so comfortable with Cole. Soon she forgot to keep her back straight so she didn't lean into Cole. Soon she forgot that they were no longer a couple.

"Do you want something else to eat or drink?"

Ava looked at the wine bottle and saw it sat empty on the table. She didn't recall drinking a lot, but then again, her glass never seemed to be empty. Maybe she needed to drink something other than wine.

"I'll have some water, thanks."

"Okay, be back in a minute."

As he walked out of the room, Ava couldn't get over how domestic they seemed. Like a real married couple.

Is this what it would've been like if they'd stayed together? Friday nights home, sitting together watching television. Or would they have been out on the town at some charity event? What if Cole had to be somewhere tonight but he'd put it off to spend the evening with her? She wasn't sure that would be the case; after all, he'd left her alone last night.

"What are you thinking so hard about?"

Cole placed a glass of cold water on the table.

"Oh, nothing. Well, actually," she paused and picked the glass, taking a small swallow. "Did you have anywhere you needed to be tonight?"

"No," he smiled ruefully. "For once I didn't have to be anywhere. Besides, even if I had an engagement, you'd be coming with me."

"Oh."

The prospect of attending events with him hadn't even crossed her mind. To her, they were simply going to be working together and living in the same house.

"You sound surprised."

"Well yes, I am. I hadn't given it much thought, to be honest. I mean, I know before I left we had a pretty busy social life, but I figured this was simply a working arrangement. It's not like this is a reconciliation or anything."

Cole reached over and turned the television off. "Would a reconciliation be a bad thing?"

"Are you for real?" she asked incredulously.

Of course reconciling would be a bad thing. They didn't have anything in common. When she'd initially walked out, people told her to just talk to Cole. Communication between couples was the lifeblood of any relationship. But she'd closed off all lines of communication when she'd fallen into her depression. Talking with Cole about what she was feeling and thinking seemed impossible to her. A bridge she couldn't cross.

Time apart had helped her work through her thoughts and doubts. She was a grown woman who, prior to Cole, had been confident and happy in her own skin. Living in Cole's world even for the short time before they'd got married had been a whole new world. A world so out of her stratosphere she'd always felt more like an intruder than a real member. No matter how many times Cole told her she was who he wanted to be with, she still expected the phone call that he was breaking up with her.

"Yes, I'm for real. I don't understand why you think working at giving our marriage another go would be such a bad thing."

"Because it would never work between us, Cole. It didn't the first time around. What makes you think we'd be any more successful this time?"

Cole turned and took hold of her hands. She wanted to yank them out of his grip. She couldn't think properly when he touched her. Her brain seemed to forget all rational thought, focus on the sensations of his warmth holding her. The way his hands had always worked magic on her. Turning her into a puddle of mush and willing to do anything he wanted.

"We didn't really give our marriage a good chance the first time around, did we?"

She couldn't deny that his words held some truth. But they wouldn't have married if she hadn't been pregnant. If only they'd waited until she'd reached the second trimester of her pregnancy. If only he hadn't rushed them into walking down the aisle. If only things had turned out differently.

"Even if we did, it wouldn't have worked out. We should've never got married in the first place."

CHAPTER 10

Cole stood up and started pacing around the room. He and Ava needed to have this conversation. They should've had it long ago. If they had, maybe they wouldn't be in this situation now.

"You regret marrying me, Ava? Is that what you're saying?" He kept his tone even, managing to keep the anger at bay.

He rested his hand on brick mantle below the television, right next to a photo that had been taken at one of the first events they'd attended together. Looking at it now, seeing the way Ava was smiling up at him, like he was the most amazing person she knew, he couldn't, no; he wouldn't believe she regretted their marriage.

"I'm not saying I regret it. But I can't help thinking of that old saying *marry in haste, repent at leisure.* Perhaps we shouldn't have rushed down the aisle. Perhaps we should've taken a little more time to get to know each other."

"I didn't need any more time. We had been seeing each other for quite a few months before we married. I wouldn't say we rushed into marriage."

He recalled the moment Ava announced they were going to have a baby. Initially he'd been shocked. Wondering how on earth it had happened, considering they'd been so careful. But then again, he knew accidents occurred and the idea of settling down and becoming a father appealed to him.

Prior to meeting Ava, he'd been getting jaded with the women parading themselves in front of him. Then, like a breath of fresh air, Ava crossed his path. He'd known the moment he'd seen her he'd wanted her. And nothing and no one would stand in his way.

"We can't change the past, Cole. But we can ensure the future is the right one for both of us. Maybe staying together isn't the right future for us."

The last thing Cole would accept was a failed marriage. He never failed at anything. He knew, given time, he could make Ava realize they belonged together, not apart.

"And maybe staying together is. We never really did give our marriage a fair go, did we?"

"Why is this so important to you, Cole?"

"Because I meant my vows when I said them. Didn't you?"

Ava opened her mouth and closed it again. For the first time since they started this conversation, Cole wondered if Ava really did want their marriage to end. The thought hadn't even crossed his mind. Some would say he was stupid to believe he and Ava belonged together. However, he truly believed in their marriage and that they were meant for each other.

Some would tell him he loved Ava. He would call it compatibility with a healthy dose of sexual attraction. His parents had let the world believe they were in love and were soul mates. But he knew differently. He knew his father had an affair and his mother had forgiven him. For some reason they had decided to stay together. In the end, they'd reached a compatibility where they'd admired and cared deeply for each other. It couldn't have been love, because if what they'd truly shared had been love, his father wouldn't have strayed from his mother's side.

The thought of kissing, let alone making love to, another woman repulsed him. The thought of another man touching Ava caused a red haze to cloud his vision. No one touched Ava but him.

"Yes, Cole. I meant my vows too."

Relief swept through him at her declaration. He could see the strain on her face. They'd talked enough about their relationship for the evening. They still had a lot of things to sort out, but they had time. Time to deal with each issue. He had no plans of giving up.

"Why don't we try and watch a movie again?" he suggested.

"I'm really tired. I think I might go to bed."

He could see her tiredness in the slump of her shoulders. He walked toward her and framed her face in his hands.

"Okay, we'll talk tomorrow." He closed the distance between them. "Goodnight, sweetheart." Her lips were pliable under his. He tasted the wine on her lips. He widened his stance; sinking his fingers into her hair, deepening the kiss. When her arms crept up around his shoulders, he pulled her even closer. His body reacted to having her close again. His cock hardened, urging him to lower Ava to the couch and take her. He'd missed her touch. Her taste. Her presence in his life.

A part of his brain still had the sense to halt things before they went too far and he didn't push her down on the couch.

"Sweet dreams," he said, as he placed a soft kiss on her cheek. "I'll see you in the morning. Don't forget to turn your alarm clock off."

He walked out of the room, heading for his own room to have a cold shower.

A gentle tapping on the door penetrated Ava's sleep. She groaned, wanting to roll over and go back to sleep. It had taken her a long time to fall asleep even though she had been exhausted. Cole's kiss had fired her neurons to life and as she watched him walking out of the room she'd wanted to chase after him. Continue with their kiss. She shouldn't be feeling this way. But their conversation had unlocked the memories of the good times of the relationship. The times where Cole had made her feel the center of his universe. It had also unlocked the dark time of their relationship. The time she wasn't ready to examine.

Another knock sounded. Whoever was responsible for waking her up wasn't going to go away.

"Come in." She called, as she sat up and pushed her hair off her face.

"Good morning, I brought you some breakfast."

Cole walked into her room, a tray balanced on one hand. He wore low-slung board shorts and nothing else. His hair, damp and slicked back off his face, indicating he'd had an early morning swim.

Ava enjoyed watching his progress toward her. His muscles bunching and stretching with each step he took. When he placed the tray on her bed she immediately grabbed the glass of juice and took a long swallow, moistening her parched throat.

"Morning," she croaked out, once she felt she had the ability to talk again.

"How did you sleep?"

"Okay. Took me a while to get to sleep."

"Really?" He smiled at her confession. "I had some trouble too."

Ava lowered her head, her hair falling over her face. She hoped it covered the blush she could feel rising up her neck.

He leaned casually against her bedside table while she started on the bowl of fresh fruit.

"Is there anything you would like to do today?"

What she really wanted to do was go back to the Margaret River house and get the rest of her things. While all her clothes and personal items had been brought to Cole's house, she still had her main computer and client files in her office. She still had other clients that she was planning events for. Just because Cole had given her an awesome job and opportunity, she couldn't ignore her other obligations.

The last thing she wanted was for Cole to travel down with her. But she knew there would be no way he'd let her go there by herself.

"I want to go to Margaret River and get some things."

"Didn't everything get brought up here?"

"Well, all my clothes and personal items. But there are things I need in my office. Your people didn't pack up my office. I need my desktop computer."

"But you have an iPad and a laptop. Why do you need a desktop computer as well?"

"Working on a desktop is easier than the laptop when it comes to designing room layouts. I have a specific computer program I use for that task. And I like to have all my client files, past and present, nearby. I refer back to them and use various concepts for every job I do."

Cole looked behind him at the clock resting on the nightstand. "How long will it take for you to get ready?"

"About a half an hour."

"Fine. I'll meet you downstairs," he stated, as he started walking out the room.

"What makes you think I want you to come with me?"

He paused in the doorway and looked over his shoulder. "Because, sweetheart, I'm not letting you out of my sight."

With that, he continued out of the room.

Shaking her head, Ava allowed herself a little laugh. Cole had acted exactly the way she expected him to act. His actions seemed to show her he cared about her and what happened to her. She wouldn't let herself let the thought take root. It was easier to think of Cole as a block of ice. As someone who couldn't care for anyone but himself. If she let herself believe he cared for, her resolve to stay impartial to his touches would crumble. And that would be extremely dangerous.

Looking at the time, she moved the tray to the side and headed toward the bathroom. She would have to remember to pack an overnight bag. There was no way they'd be able to drive there and back in one day, not matter how much she wanted it. She knew if she asked, Cole would flatly refuse to drive back. It would be strange to spend the day and night at the house with Cole, especially after it had been her haven for so long. But she would deal with it. She had to, because when they divorced she would be staying away from anything and everything that represented Cole.

CHAPTER 11

Cole unlocked the house door and held it open for Ava to enter. Spending over three hours next to her in the car had been a sweet torture. Many times he'd wanted to reach over and take her hand. It surprised him how much he needed to have a physical connection to Ava. He'd tempered the strength of his need for Ava after the miscarriage, and schooled himself to show no want as she distanced herself. The intensity of his need to be near and touch Ava wasn't something he'd experienced for some time now. He hadn't known how to deal with it so he'd held a part of himself back from Ava. Perhaps that had been the issue between them. Certainly after her miscarriage Ava hadn't wanted him to touch her as he had done previously. The doctor had told him Ava would take time to heal, physically and emotionally after the miscarriage. He never imagined she'd turn him away, even when he wanted to hold her. Comfort her. He wondered now if she thought she wasn't attractive to him anymore because she wasn't carrying his baby. It couldn't be further from the truth. His attraction for Ava only seemed to grow the more time they spent together. Maybe for her the attraction between them had died.

Oh geez, he sounded like an insecure fool. He could imagine what the guys would say to him if they could read his mind. They'd be pulling his man card faster than he could say "hello".

He followed Ava into the house. It had been a while since he'd been here. He'd phoned her when she'd relocated to this house. The only time she'd answered his call. His plan had been to try and see if they could arrange a time for him to come and see her. The call had been an absolute disaster. They'd fought over the stupidest thing. He racked his brain to see if he could remember what it was about, but his mind drew a blank.

"It shouldn't take me long to pack up my things. We could be on the road again in a couple of hours." Ava spoke, breaking into his thoughts.

He tossed his keys on the hall table, the sound of them clattering on the wood echoing around the entryway.

The last thing he wanted to do was jump back into the car to make another three-hour journey back in the same day. "Not happening."

"Why not? If you don't want to drive, I can drive."

"Ava, why are you in such a rush? Is it the thought of staying here with me?"

"No." The word fired out of her. "I thought maybe you'd want to head back to Perth. You know, you could have a Lodge meeting for all I know."

"The only place I plan on going tonight is out to dinner at Annabel's, the new restaurant that's opened up at Willow Wood Winery. I called while you were having a shower and made a reservation."

He'd heard good things about the restaurant that had opened a couple of months ago. It had been getting rave reviews and he thought it was the perfect time to try it. It had been a long time since he and Ava had had a nice romantic dinner. He had plans to romance her this weekend. Make her remember all the good times they'd shared together.

"But I didn't bring anything suitable to wear! I wish you'd told me, Cole. You'll have to cancel."

"I've got everything covered. I organized everything and packed it for you before we left."

"When?"

"I can multitask. It didn't take anything to talk on the phone, pull things from your closet, pack a bag and put it in the car while you showered."

"You went through my things while I wasn't there?"

Her anger amused him. "Ava, it's not like we haven't shared a bedroom or anything before. You've packed for me, I simply returned the favor."

"Well, I don't like it. Don't do it again."

She turned and marched up the stairs. He crossed his arms and watched her retreat, the sway of her hips mesmerizing him. She was beautiful when she was angry. When she was laughing. When she was in throes of her orgasm. Everything about Ava was beautiful.

Turning, he headed out the front door to pick up the bags that were still in the car. Within minutes he was up the stairs, wondering which direction to head. He wasn't sure which room Ava was in. The house wasn't large, not like his house in the city. Would she have chosen to sleep in the master suite, or the smaller bedroom down the hall? He knew she wouldn't have used the downstairs bedroom. It was the perfect size for an office so it made sense she would set up her computer and things there.

He took a gamble and headed right, toward the master suite. The door was open and Ava was on her tippy toes, trying to grab something from the top shelf of the walk-in closet on the opposite side of the room. A strip of bare skin was visible from her shirt riding up as she stretched. Placing the bags on the carpet, he wandered over to where she wobbled.

"Do you need some help?"

Ava yelped and swiveled quickly, losing her balance. Cole reached out and grabbed her around the waist, bringing her flush up against him. Immediately her arms gripped his shoulders.

"You scared me, hotshot," she said, as she lightly hit him on the shoulder.

"Sorry, I didn't mean to." He really hadn't, but the fact he now had his arms around Ava meant he couldn't really be sorry he'd scared her.

She wiggled against him and he bit back a groan as his body immediately reacted to the movement. Ava stilled when she made contact with his erection.

Seduction had been his plan with this trip. He'd decided to take it slow. Not to force intimacy with Ava. But he couldn't fight it any longer. He wanted to lose himself in Ava's body. Hear her cry out her completion. Feel her body clench around his as she orgasmed. He wanted her and he was done fighting it.

"Ava," he murmured, before lowering his head and capturing her lips with his. Whether she had worked out it would be futile to fight him or she'd decided she needed this as much as he did, but she softened into his embrace, and Cole knew he wasn't going to stop with kisses.

Scooping her up in his arms, he carried her over to the bed and lay her down. He broke their connection to lean down and pull off his shoes and socks. He then got on the bed next to her again, pulling her back into his arms.

If Ava was going to fight him on this, she would've got off the bed while he was taking his shoes off. Instead, she'd taken her own shoes off and had scooted up higher on the bed so that she laid propped against the pillows.

He paused, savoring the sight of her on a bed with him again. She belonged there and nowhere else. He had to convince her of that.

Cole reached over and brushed her hair off her face, trailing a finger down her soft cheek. She turned her head toward his touch. When he reached her chin, he hooked his finger under and lifted her face so she was looking directly at him. Her green eyes had softened, the gold flecks, normally buried, burned brightly out at him.

"Are you sure?" He asked, not going into specifics as he was pretty sure Ava knew exactly what he was asking.

In answer, her hands went to her shirt and started unbuttoning it. His fingers itched to help her. Instead he watched, knowing she needed to do this. Assert herself. Show him she was one hundred percent with him on this journey.

When her fingers reached the last button, he moved closer and trailed a finger down the strip of flesh between the parted material then back up again. He gently pushed her blouse off her shoulders, smoothing it down until her arms were free. He tossed the piece of clothing on the ground. He quickly divested himself of his sweater.

He smiled at her sharp intake of breath, pleased that she liked what she saw. He was glad he'd kept up with his regular workouts.

His eyes drifted shut when Ava ran her hands up his chest, her fingers tracing the ridges. It had been so long since they'd been like this. He definitely hadn't expected this to happen so soon on this trip. It felt so right.

Unable to keep his hands off her any longer, Cole trapped her hand against his chest.

"You have no idea how much I want you, Ava. How much I've missed touching you." He cupped her breast, brushing his finger over her nipple.

"How much I've missed kissing you." He replaced his finger with his mouth and kissed her breast through the lace of her bra, his teeth nipping at her distended nipple.

He lifted his head and looked at her once again. "How much I've missed making love to you."

"I've missed you too."

He groaned at her admission. Why had he wasted so much time? Why had he let her live apart from him for so long? Why hadn't he fought harder for her? Made her understand he needed her as much as she needed him.

Cole pushed aside his regrets and questions. He had the woman he desired in his arms and he planned to show her how perfect they were for each other.

He pulled away from her, his hands moving to the waistband of his jeans where he made short work of the button and zipper, sliding them off. When her hands moved to her button, he put his hand over hers.

"No, let me."

Sliding close to her again, he kissed her again. Her mouth opened, allowing him access. He wound his arms around her back, his thumb and forefinger grasping her bra fastening. With a press, it came undone. He pulled the straps down. Ava untangled her arms from around him so that the bra could slide off.

With a quick throw, the lacy item joined the rest of the clothes on the floor. Wanting to feel her whole body against his, Cole reached between them and undid the button on her jeans. Ava moaned against his mouth as his knuckles brushed up against her sex as he lowered the zipper.

He bit back his own groan as she wiggled her hips against his aching cock to help him divest her of her jeans.

They broke the kiss, both breathless as they lay on the bed in their underwear. Her lips glistened and her breasts rose and fell with her ragged breathing. He cupped her soft, plump flesh, rubbing his thumbs over her nipples.

"Cole," she moaned out his name as her head fell back on the covers. "I need you."

He knew how much Ava enjoyed having him play with her breasts. He squeezed the flesh lightly. His body screamed at him to plunge deeply into her and release the pressure building inside of him. He ignored the urges. He wanted to take his time. Enjoy having her again.

"I know, sweetheart. I want you so badly too."

He rolled onto his back, pulling her with him so that she lay on top of him. His mouth latched onto the breast swaying tantalizingly in front of him. He swirled his tongue around her nipple.

He almost lost control when Ava rubbed herself against his erection. The fabric from their underwear causing a delicious friction. If he wasn't careful, he could end this before it actually started.

Cole couldn't wait any longer and gave her breast one last kiss before tumbling her off him and to his side. Her hair surrounded her in a sexy mess. He reached down and removed his underwear, before hooking his fingers on either side of hers and drawing them down and then off.

Ava couldn't keep still as Cole smoothed his hand up her leg. She twisted as he found her ticklish spot behind her knee. He kissed it and then kept kissing his way up until he reached her center. His mouth closed over her, sucking gently. She moaned as sensations spiraled through her. She reached down and threaded her fingers through his hair, encouraging him to keep doing what he was doing.

She gave herself over to the feelings Cole generated within her. She let all thought drain out of her mind, concentrating only on what Cole was doing. Her spine tingled with every swipe of his tongue. Her hips rose off the bed as he sucked on the ball of sensitive nerves. Heat built steadily inside her, and when his tongue delved between her folds her orgasm hit hard and fast.

With her body still vibrating her release, Cole kissed his way up her belly. His tongue swirled around her belly button. He laved each nipple before he found the sensitive spot beneath her ear. He kissed it as he rested himself between her legs. All she wanted was for him to plunge into her. Bring her back to the heights he had brought her to only moments ago.

He traced his tongue around her ear, she moaned and reached down to grab his ass, lifting her hips telling him exactly what she wanted. He shifted, and the next minute he was nudging her entrance.

"Now, Cole. Please." She whispered urgently against his ear.

"Ava, I've missed you so much," he moaned as he pushed into her.

She flinched a little at having him filling her again. He stopped, and slowly her body accommodated to the size of him inside her. She kissed him, nipping at his bottom lip. He opened up and she slipped her tongue in as he started moving.

Cole set a slow rhythm. His body moving in and out of hers, gradually picking up pace until she was, once again, grasping his ass, wanting him deeper inside her.

Time stood still as she shattered around him again. Cole plunged in and out of her a couple more times, before he shouted her name as his own orgasm ripped through him. His body jerked for what like seemed forever before he collapsed on top of her, breathing heavily in her ear.

Ava wrapped her arms tightly around him, delighting in having Cole once again so close to her.

CHAPTER 12

Ava tried to roll over, but couldn't. She was wrapped tightly in Cole's embrace as he slept heavily beside her. She turned her head and saw it was just past midnight. She'd been asleep for only a short time.

As she gazed around the room, she wondered what the hell she'd been thinking. It had only taken two days of being in Cole's company before she fell into his bed. After they'd made love earlier in the day, they'd showered and then sat out on the back terrace, talking about inconsequential things.

Dinner had been magical. Cole had focused all of his attention on to her, like he couldn't breathe without having her near him. Sexual tension had swirled around them the whole time they'd been at the restaurant. If someone had asked her what she'd eaten for her main meal she wouldn't have been able to say. That's how much Cole had owned her thoughts.

It had been inevitable that the moment they returned back to the house they'd head upstairs to ease the tension. Their clothes were strewn all over the place and at the time she hadn't cared. All she'd wanted was for Cole to be filling her again. Taking her to places where she forgot to think and the only thing she could do was feel.

Now, in the dark hours of the night, regret washed over her. They hadn't even been careful. How stupid could she have been? She didn't think it was likely she could fall pregnant and she prayed to god that she didn't. She couldn't cope with the possibility of carrying a child again. After losing her first baby, the thought of going through the range of emotions, from the excitement at finding out she was pregnant to the devastation of hearing the doctor say she'd lost the baby, left her cold.

"What's wrong, sweetheart?" A hand stroked gently up her arm, comforting her even when she didn't want it.

"What are we doing, Cole?"

He propped up on one elbow. "Well, I was sleeping but now we're talking."

Her eyes had adjusted to the darkness and she could make out his smile. For some reason his flippant attitude angered her. She sat up, pulling the sheet higher to cover her. "Don't be facetious. I can't believe we did this. It wasn't the most sensible thing to do."

She blinked rapidly as Cole turned on the bedside lamp. "I have to disagree. I think this was the most sensible thing to do. We needed to do this, Ava."

"What? How on earth did we need to have sex? We've been separated for months. I'm sure it hasn't been too much of an issue for you."

Anger flamed to life in Cole's eyes. "Are you accusing me of being unfaithful to you? I think you need to be very careful with what you're implying here."

It didn't seem unreasonable to think Cole could've spent some time in bed with another woman. It made sense, because before they got together he very much played the field. A new woman every other week. The idea that he could possibly be celibate for the six months that they'd been apart just didn't ring true to her.

"What am I supposed to think, Cole? You can't deny before we started seeing each other you had a reputation."

Cole sat up abruptly. "Let me tell you something, Ava. And you'd better listen well. I'm a man of honor. I told you last night I take my wedding vows very seriously. The whole *forsaking all others* and *until death do us part* holds a wealth of meaning to me. I've seen what cheating can do to a marriage. I'm certainly not going to do it in mine."

With that, he threw back the covers and got out of the bed. He strode out, pulling on the jeans he'd worn earlier as he went.

Ava fell back on the pillows, wondering what they were going to do next. Did she regret spending the night in Cole's arms? Did Cole regret spending the night with her?

What had he meant by seeing how cheating had ruined a marriage? She knew he hadn't been married before and she'd witnessed seeing his parents together. The love they had felt for each other was palpable, so she knew he couldn't possibly be talking about them.

Could she believe him when he'd told her he hadn't been with another woman while they'd been apart? His words held water. Why was it so impossible for her to accept his words? She hated herself for doubting him. For insinuating something so cruel.

Ava also knew she couldn't let a chasm build between them again by brushing this under the carpet. That had been their problem before. Something she now realized had pretty much been her fault. Cole had wanted her to talk about the anger and sorrow she had been feeling after losing the baby. Instead she'd shut him out and closed herself off. The main reason their marriage had collapsed had been her. She had to fix this.

Getting out of bed, she picked up Cole's shirt and put it on. His scent lingered on the collar. She inhaled deeply, knowing in that moment she wanted to be wrapped in Cole's arms, not his shirt.

Ava buttoned the shirt as she walked down the stairs. A light glowed in the living room. She headed in that direction. She walked in and saw Cole standing with a glass in one hand, the other resting on the wall beside the ceiling to floor window. He'd pulled the curtains open and seemed to be gazing out into the inky blackness of the night.

Ava got to his side and laid a hand tentatively on his back. "Cole?"

Her hand moved up and down as he sighed. "I don't want to talk anymore, Ava." He lifted his glass and took a swallow of his drink.

"I'm sorry for what I said, Cole. It was wrong and I had no place to suggest that you had been unfaithful."

"Fine."

Cole had shut down. He wasn't going to let her in. Everything in her wanted to wrap her arms around him. Take away the tension radiating out of him. Deciding to take a chance, she wrapped arms around him and laid her head against his back. He tensed even more. She wasn't giving up. She wasn't going to walk away from him.

Ava had no idea how long they stood there. Eventually Cole's body relaxed and the hand that had been resting by the window covered hers.

"You should go back to bed." Cole spoke quietly as he pulled her hands away from his belly.

"Are you coming with me?"

He turned and kissed the top of her head. "I'll be there later."

Something in his tone told her it would be much later. She opened her mouth to question him, but he placed a finger over her lip. "Go, Ava."

He walked toward the kitchen, leaving her standing alone by the window.

CHAPTER 13

Ava went over the list of people attending the event. So far they'd had a good response, even though the invites had gone out late. It seemed everyone wanted to attend a function put on by Lodge Drysor.

She put the paper down and turned her chair to look out the window. It had been nearly a week since they'd spent the weekend at the country house. Cole had been quiet while she'd packed up her equipment and some of her other personal items. Conversation had been about mundane things, like neither one of them wanted to travel down the minefield of a conversation path again.

Cole had been out most evenings, telling her he had Lodge meetings to go to. He'd looked so sexy in his dinner suit, it had taken everything in her not to go over to where he stood and kiss him senseless. She should've been glad he'd been sleeping in the master bedroom and hadn't tried to sleep with her again. She'd wanted him to. She'd stayed awake listening for his arrival home, silently begging him to come into her room. Each night she'd heard the door in the distance close.

The more she worked on this event, the more intrigued she'd become with the Freemasons and what they did. She'd read a couple of things online about the organization, but because there were so many different aspects and Lodges, she didn't know which one Lodge Drysor was part of or which constitution they followed. Who knew the society was so diversified.

The sound of the phone ringing pulled her out of her thoughts. She reached over and picked up the receiver. "Ava Vaughan speaking."

"Hi Ava, my name is Gemma Hughes, I'm a reporter with *The Daily Times* entertainment section. We would like to do a feature on the Charity Ball Lodge Drysor is sponsoring. Have you got a few minutes to answer some questions?"

"I'm not sure I can be of much help. Perhaps you need to speak to one of the actual members of the Lodge."

"Oh I plan to, but I wanted to get a woman's perspective on the event."

Something about the demeanor of the reporter didn't sit well with Ava. But she thought the best thing to do would be to answer the questions.

"Okay, what did you want to know?"

"How much time have you spent with the members of the Lodge to organize the event?"

"I've only spent time with Cole Jacobs."

"Have you had any opportunity to spend time at a Lodge Drysor meeting?"

"What has this got to do with getting a woman's perspective on the event? I think perhaps we should keep the questions to the event and not on the Lodge and Freemasonry."

"But don't you wonder what an organization of men is doing fronting a charity for homeless and at risk kids? Especially when homeless kids are disappearing off the streets every day?"

The line of questioning made Ava uncomfortable. "Look, Ms. Hughes. I don't know what you're trying to find out or what you're really trying to ask. If you don't want to ask questions directly pertaining to the event then this interview is over."

"Fine. How has it been working with your estranged husband? Society pages have been buzzing with the speculation that you're reconciling. Is there any truth in those rumors?"

Ava had had enough. This reporter was digging for something to discredit Cole and Lodge Drysor. No way was she going to say something that would jeopardize anything they were doing.

"We're done with this interview, Ms. Hughes. Goodbye." Ava hung up the phone and pushed away from her desk. She needed to let Cole know what had happened.

Picking up her tablet, she strode out of her office and down the hallway toward Cole's office.

"Is he in?" she asked Fiona.

"He's got some people with him."

"Damn, I really needed to speak to him urgently. I know all his meetings are important, but do you think I could interrupt?"

"I think that should be okay. He's with Dominic, Jude and Declan."

"Perfect. They need to hear what I have to say too. Thanks, Fiona."

"You're welcome."

Ava knocked briskly on the door then opened it. Conversation stopped as she walked into the room. "Hi, sorry to interrupt, but I think you all need to hear about the phone call I just received."

She closed the door behind her and headed over to the couches where Cole and his friends were sitting.

Cole stood as Ava reached where he sat. "What happened?" He indicated for Ava to take his seat. She smiled up at him in thanks.

"I received a phone call from a Gemma Hughes from *The Daily News*. She told me she was an entertainment reporter and wanted information about the upcoming gala event."

"What did she really want?" This question came from Dominic. Ava took notice of the way his face appeared to harden when she'd said the reporter's name.

"I take it you know of her?"

"Yes, I'm familiar with Ms. Hughes."

Interesting. It certainly didn't sound like Dominic thought too highly of Gemma.

"What did you say to her, sweetheart?" asked Cole.

"Well for one thing, finding anything out about the gala from a woman's perspective was the last thing she wanted to know. All her questions were aimed at Lodge Drysor and what it does. Had I been privy to sitting in on a Lodge meeting? And what did I think about an organization made up of men helping homeless kids when a lot of homeless kids were disappearing off the streets?"

"And what did you say to her?" Dominic asked the question again. Ava noticed that Jude and Declan were exchanging glances between themselves.

There was definitely something going on between the Lodge and this reporter. Suddenly she was extremely glad she'd discontinued the call with the woman as quickly as she had.

"I told her I hadn't attended a meeting and I failed to see how the questions she was asking related to the event. I told her if she didn't start asking questions relevant to the event I was going to terminate the phone call."

"And did she?" This time it was Jude who spoke.

"Uh, no," Ava hesitated momentarily before taking a deep breath and blurting out the last question Gemma had asked. "She wanted to know if there was any truth in the rumors that because Cole and I were working together we were reconciling."

"And you said?" Cole touched her shoulder as he asked the question.

"I told her the conversation was over and to contact the Lodge to find out any further information. Then I hung up."

Silence descended on the room. The men were looking between each other, communicating without words. Was it some secret Freemason thing? They could talk without talking at all?

Finally Cole broke the silence. "I'm sorry she contacted you but you did the right thing, Ava." He leaned down and kissed her on the cheek. This was the first time he'd kissed her since the weekend. She couldn't deny it made her feel special.

Ava let the feeling spread through her. She couldn't lie to herself any longer. She still loved Cole as deeply as she had when they'd got married. Even though her initial reason for seeing him again was to get a divorce, deep down she hadn't wanted it.

Oh, she could tell herself she'd taken his job offer because of how it would look on her résumé. Or that he agreed to her request for a divorce after the job finished. She needed to be truthful with herself. The one and only reason she had taken it was to be closer to him. She'd missed Cole so much. She'd convinced herself her love for Cole hadn't been real. It made her decision to not contact him so much easier to live with.

"Thank you." Ava looked between the men again and knew they wanted to discuss what she'd shared with them, only without her around to hear what they had to say. "I think I should leave you to discuss what I told you."

The men murmured their thanks and Cole escorted her to his office door. He stopped her from opening the door.

"You handled her perfectly, sweetheart. I know it must not have been easy for you to do that. I know how much you dislike being in a position of having to deal with the media."

Ava shrugged. "True, but ever since I started my own business I've had to deal with all aspects of the media. But Cole, it sounds like she's really after you and the Lodge. She's digging, so if there's anything you need to tell me, you'd better tell me now."

"There's nothing for you to worry about." Cole indicated the men still sitting quietly on the couches. "We've got it all under control."

CHAPTER 14

After Ava left his office, Cole headed back to where his friends sat.

"Looks like we could have a problem on our hands," Cole remarked.

"Yes. We have to make sure she doesn't somehow get an invitation to the event. Or she doesn't slip past security." Dominic slammed his fist down on the table. "We don't need to have a reporter sniffing around when there is a ship is in town. We've already received information from the police that, despite all our efforts, some kids are disappearing off the streets."

"Why do you think she's targeting us?" Jude asked. "It seems very personal."

Cole nodded. "Yes, and do we know why an entertainment reporter is digging into us?"

"I have no idea but I plan to get to the bottom of it." Dominic stood. "Trust me, I will find everything out about her and she will regret ever coming after Lodge Drysor."

As his friends walked out, Cole knew Dominic well enough to know that Gemma Hughes should be very worried she'd poked the bear. He wouldn't like to be in her shoes.

Cole went back to his desk and dragged his laptop closer to him. He searched out the reporter's name on the internet. A string of articles popped up on the screen. Most were related to social events she'd covered. Not one was an investigative piece.

Something wasn't right with this reporter. Her threat to expose some dark secret at the gala needed to be treated seriously, considering her attempt to ply Ava for information.

He knew he could dig further but saw no point. Dominic, as the Right Worshipful Master of the Lodge, would do everything necessary to protect the integrity of Lodge Drysor and their activities; the ones the public knew about and the ones they didn't.

His phone rang and as he answered it, he forced thoughts of the threatening email and the reporter who sent it from his mind. He still had half a workday to attend to.

Cole walked into the kitchen of his house. The aroma of garlic and the distinctive scent of tomatoes greeted him. His stomach grumbled in appreciation. Ava, earbuds in and her body swaying to rhythm she was listening to, stood stirring a pot of whatever was giving the kitchen its warm aroma.

He took a moment to take the scene in. This is what he'd wanted when he'd married Ava. To see her happy and relaxed and cooking in their kitchen. A home-cooked meal to come home to.

It hit him how much he'd missed having her close. They may be living in the same house again, but they continued to live separate lives. Like they had after Ava had lost the baby.

Ever since their weekend away, they hadn't spent much time together. They'd been traveling to work separately. Cole had been out most evenings because of Lodge meetings. Tonight there wasn't one, and when Fiona had mentioned Ava had left early, he'd quickly finished what he had been doing and left the office.

After seeing her in his office and touching her, he wanted to spend as much time as possible with her.

Giving into the desire to kiss the exposed flesh of her neck, Cole walked over to where Ava stood. Leaning in, he slipped his arms around her waist and kissed her neck. Her skin was warm and tasting faintly of the ingredients of the sauce she was making.

She turned her head quickly, bringing her lips tantalizingly close to his. Shock had her green eyes wide and bright. She looked so beautiful with her hair scraped back in a messy ponytail, strands escaping from the elastic binding.

"Cole, you scared me. I didn't expect you home so soon."

Instead of answering, Cole twisted her around so she was facing him, closed the distance between their mouths, and locked his lips on hers. She'd been sampling the sauce, the taste of tomatoes lingered on her mouth.

God, it felt so good to have in his arms again. To have her arms around him again. Her lips on his.

As she moaned, he knew she'd missed this as much as he had. His hands roamed the back of her soft sweater until he reached the hem. Lifting it, he brushed his fingers against the small of her back. He trailed his fingers up her spine, enjoying the feel of the shiver as it rippled through her body.

About to lift her sweater so that he could sample her sweet breasts, something hot landed on his neck.

"Ouch. What the hell is that?"

Hearing Ava giggle was unexpected. She leaned back and held up the spoon she had been using to stir the pot when he'd come up and kissed her.

"I forgot I had this in my hand," she said, leaning past him to rest it on a spoon holder. Then her hand brushed against something in his hair. "I think you got some sauce on you, hotshot."

She was laughing now as she showed him her finger covered in tomato sauce. Cole gripped her hand and brought her finger closer to his mouth. His body hardened even further as he sucked the sauce off. He kept his eyes locked on hers, watching as they widened even further at his action.

This time Ava took the initiative and instigated a kiss between them when he relinquished her finger. It only took seconds for them to be caught up in the explosive passion that had once burned fiercely between them.

Ava pushed his jacket off and loosened his tie as his hands delved beneath her sweater again, this time pushing it up so that he could whisk it off her.

Soon his shirt and tie joined her sweater on the ground. Cole was lost with need to have Ava again. His fingers found the clasp of her bra and deftly undid it. His hands came around to her front to cup her breasts.

Ava gasped and pulled her mouth away from his, allowing him to sample her beautiful breasts.

He took a nipple in her mouth and sucked on it gently. Her hips mirrored his action, brushing up against his straining erection.

"Cole," she moaned, her fingers digging into his scalp, keeping him close to her breasts.

"I know, sweetheart," he whispered against her breast. "I know. I need you too." His hands moved to undo the button of her jeans when an alarm buzzed loudly in the kitchen. He wrapped his arms around her, instinctively protecting her from the sound. "What is that?"

"That," Ava sighed, "is the timer telling me I need to check the garlic bread."

Ava quickly untangled her from his arms and bent down to pick up her sweater. Her jeans stretched and cupped her ass perfectly. His cock pulsed at the sight, wanting a sweet release.

As she slipped her sweater over her head, hiding her beautiful, creamy skin from him, Cole knew their little tryst in the kitchen was over.

"How long until dinner?" he asked as he bent and scooped up his own discarded clothes.

"You're not going out?" Ava asked as she closed the over door, turned the temperature down and set the timer again.

"Nope, I'm all yours tonight." Cole ran his fingers through his hair and connected with the sticky mess left from the spilt sauce. "Do I have time to have a shower?"

"You're joining me for dinner?"

She seemed surprised at his question.

"Yep, so I ask again, do I have time for a quick shower or is dinner ready to be served?"

"Ummm yep, I'll keep everything turned down low so it doesn't spoil." She crossed her arms across her chest, squashing her breasts together, tempting him to tell her to turn everything off and join him in the shower.

Deciding not to push things, Cole brushed passed her, smiling at her short intake of breath. "I'll be back before you know it."

Ava gripped the counter and took a couple of deep breaths as she watched Cole's retreating back. She gazed around the kitchen and wondered if she'd imagined the intense, passionate embrace they'd shared.

Her fingers touched her lips, feeling their slight puffiness; she had her proof right there.

The sauce popping drew her attention back to the task at hand. She hoped Cole was going to be happy with a dinner of pasta and spicy tomato sauce with garlic bread. She'd expected him to follow his normal routine of coming home, changing into a suit and going out the door. She'd got used to preparing meals for one. She'd made extra today so she could put the leftover in the freezer and have it at a later date.

With economical movements she drained the pasta, shaking off the excess water, before distributing it evenly into two bowls. She poured the tomato sauce over the top and then added some grated cheese. By the time she had the bowls ready, the timer sounded and Cole walked into the kitchen, bringing his clean, musky scent. His hair, damp from his shower, was slicked back, enticing her to run her fingers through it to mess it up.

He smiled his lazy grin. "Perfect timing. What can I help you with?"

Needing to get him out of the kitchen, she pointed to the bowls and silverware sitting on the countertop. "You can take those to the table while I cut the bread and put it on a plate."

"I can do that."

Cole picked up the bowls and rounded the bench to place them on the table sitting in the little nook created by the bay window. He seemed so relaxed. The scene so very domestic that if she wasn't careful, Ava could imagine a future of them eating dinner together in the cute little nook.

The image unsettled her. Neither one had talked of what was going to happen after the gala. Did they have a future together? Did she want to try again with Cole?

CHAPTER 15

Sipping the wine Cole had opened for dinner, Ava rested her feet on the coffee table as she flicked through the channels on the television. Cole was cleaning up the kitchen. He'd admonished her when she jokingly asked if he knew how to stack the dishwasher. Then he informed her his mother had equipped him with all the necessary skills to look after himself.

She'd laughed and figured that she'd check the counters before she used them tomorrow morning to make breakfast.

"Find anything exciting to watch?"

Cole came into the room carrying a tray that had a coffee pot, cups and some chocolate biscuits on a plate.

"Hmm, who knew my hotshot was so domesticated."

Cole laughed and dropped a kiss on her nose. "Don't let the guys know. They'd tease the hell out of me if they knew."

Ava crossed her chest in the age-old action of swearing to never spill a secret. "Your domestic abilities are safe with me. I won't tell a soul."

Cole settled on the couch next to her, his arm closed over her shoulders. Instead of holding herself stiff in his embrace, she curled into his side, tucking her legs up beside her.

"What happened after I left you and Dominic and the others in the office?" His remark about not telling the guys had reminded her of the encounter with the reporter and her telling the guys about it.

"Not much. Dominic is going to look into it."

Ava lifted her head from his chest and looked at him. "What aren't you telling me?"

A heavy sigh rippled through him, as if he was warring with himself about whether he should tell her what he knew. Or keep it to himself.

She decided to alleviate his uncertainty. "Whatever you say will stay between us."

Cole's hand closed around her head, encouraging her to lay her head back on his chest. "Dominic and I and the others were meeting to discuss an email she'd sent to the four of us."

"What did it say?"

"She alluded to having some information about the business the Lodge was carrying on and implied she would expose it at the gala."

"Did everyone who's a member of the Lodge get it?"

"No, only us four."

"Why you four?"

"Because Dominic, Jude and Declan hold the main offices in the Lodge."

"Do you hold an office? Is that why you got it as well?"

Cole took a sip of his wine before answering. "Yes. I currently hold the office of Senior Deacon."

"What does a *Senior Deacon* do?" She looked up at him with a cheeky smile. "Do you hold the billy goat?" She couldn't help but refer to the conversation they'd had the first night she came back to live in the house. This time she wasn't saying it to hurt him.

Cole laughed and brushed a hand down her head. "No. Basically my principle duties are to deal with the candidates during certain ceremonies. I take them around the Lodge room and speak for them during the ceremonies."

Ava couldn't help but wonder what happened at the ceremonies he talked about. She wanted to ask, but she decided to let it pass for the moment.

"So why did you get the email then? Still doesn't make sense if your position isn't really one of power, like the others?"

"It's common knowledge that the four of us are not only Freemasons and business associates. We're all friends, and more too."

"What do you mean more? You've never really explained the relationship between the four of you."

Cole took the remote out of her hand and turned the television off. She hadn't even noticed the sound it was making. All her focus had been on Cole and hearing him talk. It was nice to sit and talk with him.

"Well, Dominic and Jude are cousins. Dominic and I have been friends for years because both our fathers were Freemasons, although they weren't members of Lodge Drysor, or even the same Lodge. The Lodge Dom and I are members of came about when our original Lodges merged together. And Jude and Declan are best friends."

Her head reeled with the information but she thought she had it straight in her mind. "So let me get this straight, your father and

Dominic's father knew each other through Freemasonry but they weren't in the same Lodge."

"Right."

"So how did they get to be friendly then?"

"Well, they visited each other's Lodges and attended meetings like I do. There were often combined events with all the different Lodges that our fathers went to and they took us. The kids tended to hang out with each other and so Dom and I became friends that way. Then when we joined our own separate Lodges we became better friends."

"What about Jude and Declan? Were their fathers Freemasons too?"

"Jude's was but Declan's dad died when he was young, and so he tended to hang around Jude's all the time and saw Jude's dad get ready. Declan found the organization interesting so he asked Jude's father if only sons of Freemasons could be a member, or if anyone could." Cole reached out and took a biscuit off the plate, finishing it in two bites before he continued talking. "Jude's father always considered Declan as his surrogate son so he introduced him as a prospective candidate."

"So you don't have to be related? Anybody off the street can join?"

"Pretty much. But you have to have a genuine interest in becoming a Freemason. It's not something to be taken lightly."

"I'm beginning to see that." Ava reached over to the coffee pot and poured herself a cup. The aroma of the freshly brewed beverage tantalized her nostrils. "There is a lot more to Freemasonry that just the silly talk of secret handshakes, sacrificing virgins and other stuff."

"Oh, there's a secret handshake all right, but the other stuff is mostly myths made up to make it seem more sinister than it really is."

They sat quietly for a few more minutes, content to be with each other.

"This is nice," Cole murmured as he placed a soft kiss on her cheek. "I like holding you. Talking to you."

"Me too. We never did it enough before, did we? Oh I mean we talked, but we didn't talk, talk. You know, where we shared what we were really thinking and feeling."

Cole breathed out, feathering through her hair. "No we didn't. Perhaps we should have."

"Maybe."

Although if they'd spent evenings like this, would Cole have got bored with her and discarded her, like he had so many women before her? It was something she didn't want to ask and spoil the serenity of their evening.

"I'm sorry that reporter tried to drag you into whatever she's trying to dig up."

"It's fine. Is there anything to be worried about with her? Do you think she will turn up at the gala and cause problems?"

"We don't know, but we're not going to take any chances. I've already arranged extra security and Dominic is looking into it.

He is far from happy with this woman threatening not only the Lodge, but our charity as well. He's determined to get to the bottom of it."

Ava shuddered. The last thing she would ever want would to get on the bad side of Dominic. "I shouldn't feel this way, but I pity that girl if Dominic ever has a face to face meeting with her."

Cole's laughed, the sound rumbling beneath her ear. "Me too. But if I know Dominic, he'll do anything possible to keep from causing a scene at such an important event."

"I'm sure," she murmured. "It's not too far away. Hopefully he'll sort everything out by then."

"He will." Cole took hold of her mug and she relinquished it. He placed it on the table. "I'm done talking. Let's go to bed."

Ava had no doubt he meant for them to go to bed together, not separately. She couldn't lie to herself. After they'd almost made love in the kitchen, her body had been aching to be filled by Cole again. She wasn't planning on saying no tonight.

She reached up and cupped his cheek. The light shading of stubble from his five o'clock shadow prickled beneath her palm. "Let's."

Cole stood and bent down to pick her up. Ava closed her arms around him and buried her head into his neck, sniffing deeply. He smelled so good. This was where she belonged. Here, in Cole's house and in his arms.

CHAPTER 16

Ava secured the back of the emerald earrings Cole had given her and gave her reflection a final once-over. Her green dress complemented the earrings beautifully. She lightly touched the stone, thinking about when she'd worn them to ask Cole for a divorce. At the time she'd told herself it was to prove that she was over him and could wear them without thinking back to the day they'd committed their lives to each other. But perhaps, subconsciously, that had been the main reason she'd worn them. To remind Cole what they once had and maybe could again. Even though a reconciliation had been the farthest thing from her mind that night.

Now look at her. She'd moved into Cole's house and had moved into his bedroom. After the night when they'd had a quiet dinner and had spent time talking, Cole had told her, after bringing her to the most amazing climax, that she was moving into his bedroom. She had agreed and hadn't regretted the decision at all.

"You look beautiful, sweetheart."

Lost in her thoughts, she hadn't been aware of Cole coming up behind her. She smiled at him in the reflection, taking in how sexy he looked in his tuxedo. The same one he'd been wearing that night, only a short month ago.

"You don't look half bad either, Mr. Jacobs."

"Only half bad? Them's fighting words, Mrs. Jacobs."

Mrs. Jacobs. It was the first time he'd called her that since their wedding day. The doctors had called her Mrs. Jacobs at the hospital.

We're sorry, Mrs. Jacobs, but I'm afraid you've lost your baby. There was nothing we could do to stem the bleeding. It's what we call a spontaneous abortion. Nature's way of dealing with an unviable fetus.

She'd hated anyone calling her Mrs. Jacobs afterwards. It always reminded her of the doctor's words. To her, it wasn't an *unviable fetus*, it was her baby. Her and Cole's son or daughter. She'd pushed Cole away after that.

Tears welled up in Ava's eyes and she turned away from the mirror so that she could face Cole. She clutched at the lapels of his jacket. The time had come to forget associating her being called *Mrs. Jacobs* with that time. She should be proud to be called Mrs. Jacobs. Proud to be Cole's wife.

"I'm sorry, Cole," she whispered. "I'm so sorry."

Cole put down the box he held in his hand and wrapped his arms around Ava, trying to comfort her. He was at a complete loss as to why the tears had started to build in her eyes, making the green of her irises glow brightly.

He lifted her face and gently wiped away the tears with his thumbs. "What are you sorry for, sweetheart?"

"For pushing you away after I lost the baby. It was cruel and awful of me to do that."

"Oh sweetheart, you were hurting so badly. I'm sorry I couldn't take away the pain."

"No, you tried everything to help me, Cole. But I was too selfish. I believed you couldn't possibly understand what I was going through. I thought, 'I'm the one that suffered the loss, not you; you couldn't feel the depth of pain that I felt'. Please forgive me for being so selfish."

He captured her hand and held it against his cheek. "Shhh, it's okay. There's nothing for me to forgive. It was a horrible, tragic situation."

"I hated that doctor for what he said."

Cole tensed when he heard that. He'd been chased out of the emergency trauma room shortly after they'd got to the hospital. He hadn't wanted to leave but the nurses had insisted he go. They told him Ava wouldn't want him to see them examine her. The pain in Ava's eyes as they ushered him out of the room so he could complete some paperwork was a sight he hadn't forgotten very quickly.

"What did the doctor say? Dammit, I knew I should've demanded to stay with you while they examined you."

Ava shook her head against him. "It wouldn't have made any difference if you'd stayed or not. The baby was already gone." She laughed harshly. "A spontaneous abortion. Nature's way of dealing with an unviable fetus."

Anger boiled inside of him. How could a doctor, a person who'd taken an oath to protect and do the best for patients, tell a grieving mother her child was an *unviable fetus*. "That was our son or daughter he was talking about. How could he say something so cruel?"

He let go of Ava, too angry to be able to comfort her. He needed to move to work out the anger. "There's no way I would've let him get away with that if I was in the room with you."

This time it was Ava who reached out to comfort Cole. "Cole, honey, it's okay. I shouldn't have told you."

"What you should've done was told me the minute I walked back into that room," he said vehemently.

"Stop, Cole. There's nothing we can do about it now. You can't get angry now. There's no point. Tonight is not the night to get into it. It's too important to you and the Lodge."

He scrubbed a hand down his face and blew out a breath, consciously relaxing his shoulders. "You're right, there's nothing we can do. It's in the past." He walked back toward where Ava stood, still by the mirror. He cupped her face and kissed her softly on the lips. "I'm sorry too."

Ava smiled sweetly and he had to stop himself from scooping her up and placing her on the bed, gala event be damned.

"I know what you're thinking, but let's save it for later."

Desire flared even brighter within him. "I'll be holding you to that."

"I can't wait," she murmured, and then looked at the black box he'd placed on the dresser. "Is that for me?"

"Maybe," he teased, and then laughed out loud at the look she sent him. He held up his hands in surrender. "Okay, okay. Yes, it is for you."

He leaned past her, making sure his shoulder brushed her breast. He bit back a smile at her inhalation of breath.

"What is it?"

He traced the low neckline of her dress. "Do you have a necklace you're planning to wear?"

Confusion crossed her face. "Why do you want to know what jewelry I'm wearing? I haven't decided."

Cole opened the box. "How about wearing this?" He pulled out the matching necklace to the earrings he'd given to her as a wedding gift to wear the day they married. The large emerald stone, surrounded by small bright white diamonds, was suspended from a thick gold chain.

"It's beautiful, Cole," she whispered. He spied tears, once again, shimmering in her eyes. "I'd be honored to wear it."

He undid the clasp and Ava turned to allow him to put it on. When the task was completed she turned back to him, her hand gently touching the stone. It accentuated her V-neck of her dress perfectly, sitting just above the curve of the top of her breasts.

"It looks stunning, sweetheart."

Ava turned back to look at herself in the reflection, her eyes glassy with unshed tears. She took a deep breath and one tear trickled down her cheek. He turned her back to face him wiped away the tear.

"Hey, I wanted to make you smile, not make you cry."

She laughed. "Happy tears. I'm not sure I deserve something so lovely."

"You've done an amazing job at pulling this charity event together. It looked like a complete disaster before you got here. We are very appreciative of all that you've done."

The light died in her eyes. "So this is just a thank you gift then?"

"In a way, but it's definitely more than just a thank you gift."

If possible, Ava's spine straightened even more and remoteness seemed to engulf her. "Then what is it?"

Somehow, the gift of giving the necklace he'd had made to give to her on their first anniversary had taken a sudden U-turn. Sure, their anniversary had passed before she'd approached him for a divorce. Tonight had seemed the perfect night to give it to her. Telling her it was a thank you gift probably wasn't his smartest move. He couldn't change his words. He opened his mouth to speak, but Ava held up her hand.

"No, Cole, don't say anything. Not if it's taking you this long to think of something to say to me." She picked up her purse from the table and brushed past him. "We're going to be late if we don't leave now."

Cole watched her retreating back and wondered how something as simple as giving a gift had turned into such a disaster.

CHAPTER 17

Ava's mouth ached. Forcing herself to smile as if she hadn't a care in the world was taking its toll. She took a sip of her sparkling water and scanned the room to see if she could see Cole. Although she had no idea why she wanted to see him. Not after giving her a beautiful necklace and saying it was a thank you gift. Her heart had hoped it was sign he loved her. That he wanted her to stay with him after the gala.

"Ava?"

Ava turned to the person who'd spoken her name. "Hi Dominic." He looked handsome in his tuxedo too. To her he didn't look as handsome as Cole did, but she was sure to someone else he probably did.

"On behalf of all the brethren of Lodge Drysor, I'd like to thank you for pulling together this evening. It's our most successful one yet."

"I'm happy to hear it's doing well. It's a good charity to raise funds for. I'm pleased to be a part of it."

"We're pleased to have you on our team. I hope to see you around at other functions."

The thought of seeing Cole at events and not being able to be close to him, or worse, seeing him with another woman, wasn't something she really wanted to contemplate at this moment.

"I'm not sure if that will happen."

Dominic raised his eyebrow. "Why?"

Ava bristled at Dominic's autocratic tone. "I fail to see how it's any of your business what I do or where I go."

"No, you're right, it's not. But Cole is my friend and he's been a different person since you came back to work on this event."

Ava's interest was piqued at Dominic's comment. "How has he been different?"

He shrugged. "He's been happier. More content. He's lost the air of sadness that surrounded him since the day you left."

Cole had been sad? "I'm not sure how true that is. But it doesn't matter. I'm not really in the mood to discuss Cole or how he has changed."

"Fair enough." He gave her outfit the once over. "May I compliment you on your dress? It's a beautiful color on you."

Ava felt her cheeks heat. "You may and thank you." She cleared her throat. There was no point taking her agitation at Cole out on Dominic. It wouldn't hurt her to be friendly with him. "Are you here with anybody this evening, Dominic?"

She could imagine the sort of woman gracing Dominic's arm. She'd be exactly like the women Cole had been seen with before they'd got together.

"No. Going solo this evening." He gazed around the room as if looking for someone. The concept of a man as good looking as Dominic being here alone seemed extremely unusual. It made her think about the reporter. Had he come alone in case she turned up and he hadn't wanted to be encumbered with a date, should he need to take some action?

"Did you find out anything more about the reporter who contacted me?"

"Yes."

His tone suggested he wouldn't answer any further questions about the woman. What had he found?

Ava gave herself a mental shake. It didn't matter if Dominic had found out she was related to the Queen of England. It didn't concern her at all.

She spared a glance at her watch. She needed to check in with the hotel event coordinator to make sure the meals would be served soon. "If you'll excuse me, Dominic. I need to check in and make sure we're running to schedule."

"By all means."

As she walked away a hand touched her arm, halting her departure. She looked at Dominic. "Was there something else?"

"I wanted to say that I hope things between you and Cole are working out. With you wearing the pendant he'd had made for you for your first wedding anniversary, I'm hopeful you've worked everything out. Thanks again for organizing this event, Ava."

He released his hold on her arm and turned around to walk away.

Ava stood there speechless, her fingers touching the emerald resting against her skin. It was an anniversary gift? Why hadn't Cole told her that? Why had he said it was thank you gift?

She quelled the urge to stamp her foot in frustration. The man was impossible. If he'd told her it was an anniversary gift, things could've been so different.

Really? You were looking to find a fault in him again. Something to prove to you that he was getting ready to dump you and move onto the next pretty woman. When are you going to stop letting your insecurities rule your life?

Ava ignored the voice inside her head and the lecture it was giving. Had she been wrong about Cole all along? Was there a chance he did actually love her?

"The event is lovely, Cole. Ava did a wonderful job."

Cole smiled at his mother. "Yes, she did. I'm very proud of her."

"If that's the case, then why are you standing here with me and not with her?"

His mother was giving him a look that transported him back to being ten years old and she'd discovered his pet frog in the bathtub. "We've been together."

His mother laughed. "You walked in together and spent about ten minutes standing awkwardly next to each other." She placed a hand on his arm. "You want to tell me what's going on?"

Having a deep and meaningful conversation with his mum at a charity event wasn't high on his list of things to do tonight. "Everything is fine."

"Cole, do not lie to your mother," she admonished him. "You don't have to go into a lot of a detail, but answer me this question. Do you love Ava?"

He looked around the room and saw Dominic talking to Ava. His protective instincts kicked in when he saw them together. He knew Dominic could be pretty intimidating and he didn't want Ava to feel uncomfortable. He relaxed when he saw them smile. He would do anything to protect Ava. Keep her safe. He couldn't imagine living without her. He'd hated being apart from her. For someone who ran a multimillion dollar company, he should've been confident in dealing with his wife. Unfortunately, he wasn't. He was a novice; Ava generated feelings in him he'd never experienced before. Feeling vulnerable wasn't something he wanted to acknowledge.

He remembered watching her walk down the aisle toward him in her wedding dress. How beautiful she looked. How everyone in attendance faded to nothing when she stood beside him. The way his hand tingled when she touched him. How immensely proud he'd felt when the minister announced them man and wife. He'd wanted to shout to everyone there Ava was his and no one else's.

His wife.

His life.

His love.

"Yes," he turned and looked at his mother. "Yes, I love her."

"Then fight for her. Whatever is going on between the two of you, love can conquer." His mother touched his cheek in the loving gesture only a mother can generate. "You had so much to deal with at the beginning of your marriage, it was no wonder it wobbled. But love is worth fighting for. No matter how bad the situation that has led to troubled times."

"Including cheating?" Cole wished he hadn't said anything when the color drained from his mother's face. "I'm sorry, don't answer that."

His mother was a woman who didn't back down from anything, and as she cleared her throat, he knew she wasn't about to back down now either.

"Yes, Cole, even cheating." She looped her arm through his. "As you said, this isn't the best place for this conversation but we need to have it tonight. Let's find a quiet place to talk."

Cole put his hand over his mother's and led her out of the ballroom. There were tables and couches set up in the foyer of the ballroom. He found a table in the corner and seated his mother before taking the seat opposite her. He wasn't sure he really wanted to hear what she had to say, but perhaps he needed to hear this to move on. Find out why his mother took his father back after he'd had a month-long affair.

"I didn't realize you know about your father's affair. How did you find out?"

Cole sighed. "I heard you and Dad arguing. You didn't know I'd come downstairs to get something to eat. I had my headphones on but it was between songs when I heard you asking Dad about his *whore*."

His mother closed her eyes. "I'm sorry. I'm so sorry you had to hear that."

"I can't say I was happy about it, and for a long time I hated him and what he'd done to you."

"Yes, I recall you were surly with him for quite a while. I have to admit I was so caught up in working to save my marriage that I simply assumed it was hormones making you sullen and moody with your father." She smiled at him. "You were so sweet with me."

"I wanted to punish him for making you sad. I still don't understand why you took him back. But then he introduced me to Freemasonry and, even though I never forgot what he did, I figured I could forgive him if you did. Plus I really did enjoy the time we spent together driving to meetings."

"I'm glad that you were able to move forward. Your father treasured the time you spent together and he was incredibly proud of your achievements within Freemasonry." Tears sparkled in her eyes. "I'm sure he's boasting in heaven saying it's his son and his friends who are ensuring Freemasonry doesn't die. You and the others have taken a charity that was on the verge of closing to one of the strongest in the city."

If only his mother knew exactly what the charity did.

"This still doesn't tell me why you forgave him, Mum."

"Oh Cole, darling, it's quite simple. I loved your father to distraction. So much so I started to suffocate that love with my insecurities and need to be constantly with him. Do you remember there was time there he didn't go to any meetings? I wouldn't allow him to go. So he started working later and later at the office and, well, there was a young intern who flattered him and he was so tired of fighting me, he didn't have it in him to fight her."

Cole couldn't fathom looking at another woman. Ava was his everything. He hadn't even been tempted during their estrangement, no matter how hard the women tried to tempt him. "If you both loved each other as much as you say you did, how could he bear having another woman touch him?"

His mother shrugged her shoulders. "I suspect there was a time he didn't quite like me. Anyway, I was feeling so off that I went to the doctors and found I was suffering a chemical imbalance that was affecting my hormones, which, in turn, heightened my emotions. Once I started taking medication everything became more rational again."

"Is that when you found out?"

"No, it was after I found out and I confronted your father that everything came to light."

"I don't remember you being sick. Especially not after I overheard that conversation."

"That's because you weren't here. You were doing that month-long exchange program. You went over to Japan."

Cole remembered now. At the time he'd been glad and scared to go away. Glad that he didn't have to see his dad and scared because he loved his dad and thought he'd come back and find out he'd moved out. When he'd returned, his dad was still living in the house and his parents' relationship seemed a little better. But he couldn't forget what he'd overheard, so he'd been angry with his father.

"What happened while I was away?"

"I had a series of tests and had to spend some time in hospital. What they say, about facing your own mortality changing the way you think, is true. Only it was with your father. He found out that he couldn't stand the thought of me not being in his life. He was so scared I was going to die that he didn't leave my side." She clasped her hands under her chin. "Before I ended up in the hospital I'd asked him for a divorce. But his love and support got me through my medical crisis. The whole situation made us stronger."

Cole took a deep breath. His mother had passed on a lot of information he hadn't known. If he was honest with himself, he'd pushed a lot of what he was feeling to the back of his mind. He hadn't wanted to deal with it. He was just glad his parents hadn't split up.

Time had healed his wounds with his father and, like his parents' relationship, over time Cole's relationship with his dad had only got stronger.

"True love is worth fighting for Cole. I know if you didn't love Ava as much as you do, you would've divorced her the moment she walked out." His mother reached across the table laid her hand over his. "Now, what are you going to do?"

He didn't need his mother to ask him what he planned to do. He'd known before they'd left the house tonight what he'd wanted to do. He knew what he had to do. He had to find Ava now.

He got up and walked around to where his mum sat. "Thanks, Mum. I love you."

"I love you too, son. Now go get your girl."

He smiled. "Oh, I plan to."

CHAPTER 18

"Time to leave."

Ava jumped when the words were spoken in her ear. She whirled around, her hand on her heart. "What on earth do you think you're doing, scaring me like that? Sheesh, Cole."

She had been wondering where he'd got to. She hadn't seen him since just after they'd arrived. Tension from their small disagreement had made the drive to the hotel silent. She'd been relieved when he'd gone off to speak to someone but she'd thought he'd come back and find her.

"I'm sorry, I didn't mean to scare you. It's time for us to go."

Ava took a step back, evading his attempt to take her hand. "I'm not going anywhere. And really, neither should you."

"Ava, I need to talk to you. It's important."

Dread filled her. Cole was going to tell her he'd changed his mind and would give her a divorce, just liked he'd agreed to when he'd asked her to organize this event.

"I don't want any—"

She stopped what she was saying as she heard raised voices at one of the doors to the ballroom. "What is going on?"

Ava started to make her way over to where she saw Dominic getting into an argument with a woman dressed in a midnight blue evening dress.

A hand on her arm stopped her progress. "Leave it. Dominic's got it under control."

She watched as Dominic took the woman's hand and led her out the door. It looked all very civilized, but Ava knew it was anything but.

"You don't think it's that reporter, do you?" she asked Cole.

"I'm not sure, but if it is we don't need to worry. Dominic will sort it out. Besides, look around, everyone has already forgotten about it."

Ava looked around the room at the fellow guests. They appeared to be continuing with their dancing and talking, but she had a feeling there would be plenty of discussion amongst them as to what was happening between Dominic and the woman.

Cole touched her arm. "Let's go, Ava."

His tone brooked no argument. Whatever he had to say, it was probably better that they don't create a scene at the event. "Fine."

They paused long enough for her to check in with the hotel coordinator before Cole ushered out of the hotel into their waiting car.

It took everything in her not to ask him what he wanted to talk to her about on the drive home. She didn't want to start an argument, but the silence in the car was making her tenser than a piano wire.

"Are you happy with how the evening went? Looks like a lot of money is going to the charity."

"Yes, everyone will be very pleased. I hope you were able to have a good time."

Anger flared in her at Cole's words. "If you call being left alone for most of the evening, having a good time. Then sure, I had a *fabulous* time."

"Sarcasm doesn't become you, sweetheart."

Ava clenched her fists and looked out the window, to save herself from leaning across the console and punching Cole on the arm.

The rest of the drive passed in silence and Ava only relaxed when Cole pulled into the driveway. Once he turned the engine off, she had her door open and was out of the car before the garage door had even closed. Her only goal was to go upstairs and start packing. She didn't know why, but she was convinced Cole was planning to end their marriage tonight. There'd been no more talk of reconciling since she'd moved into his room. She didn't want to assume that because they were sleeping together again, everything between them was fine.

"Where are you off to in such a hurry?" Cole asked as she raced up the stairs, high heels in her hand.

"To pack."

She yelped, as with lightning quick speed Cole had taken the steps two at a time, caught her around the waist and lifted her over his shoulder as if she were a sack of flour.

"Cole! What are you doing?" she demanded as he strode up the stairs and toward their bedroom. Once there he dumped her on the bed; leaning over, he placed an arm on either side of her.

"And pray tell, why are you packing?"

Ava scrambled back on the bed to put some distance between them. "Well, the gala is over. I've completed my part of the agreement. Now it's your turn."

Cole shed his jacket and undid his bowtie, tossing them to the ground before he sat on the bed and ran a fingertip down her ankle. "Really. And what exactly are you talking about?"

He looked like a panther on the prowl, eyeing its next conquest. But she refused to be intimidated. "Don't try and act as if you don't know what I'm talking about. But if you want, I'll play along. It's time to grant me a divorce."

"Not happening." He fired back at her as he shot off the bed. "There will be no divorce, Ava."

She moved off the bed as well. Now she stood on one side and Cole stood on the other. The bed providing a buffer between them. "Why not, Cole? Did you think just because I started sleeping with you that everything was fine between us? Nothing has changed since we got married."

"Everything has changed, Ava. I told you I wanted to try again and I thought we were doing a pretty good job of starting over. Trying to rebuild our marriage."

"What rebuilding do you see us doing?"

"This," he waved his hand around the room.

"What? You mean sleeping together?" she scoffed. "We never had any problem in that department, Cole. If fact, it was sleeping together that got us into this marriage."

"What do you mean by that?" he said quietly, striding around the bed until he stood in front of her.

"Don't you see, Cole, if I hadn't fallen pregnant we would never had a reason to get married. If only we'd waited a few more weeks before rushing down the aisle, who knows where we would've been today."

Cole took a step back like she'd punched him in the gut. "You think the only reason I married you was because you were pregnant?"

"Well, wasn't it?" She laughed harshly. "It wasn't like you loved me or anything. Not the way I love you."

His eyes flared at her declaration of love and she wanted to snatch the words back. She'd never intended for him to know she still loved him. Every time she'd told him she loved him before, he always responded with *I know you do.* Never once had he said he loved her.

"How can you be so sure I don't love you, Ava?"

His words slowed the adrenaline racing through her. She didn't want to believe what he was saying. Was he telling her that he'd loved her then and he still loved her now?

No, it wasn't possible. He was only saying that because she'd told him of her love for him. He couldn't love her. But what if he did? What if he wasn't asking the question to appease her? What if he meant it?

"What are you saying?"

Cole walked up to her. He hooked one arm around her waist, bringing her closer to him. He ran his other hand down her cheek. "I'm saying that I didn't marry you because you were pregnant. I married you because I wanted to. I married you because, with you, life is amazing. I married you because I loved you then and I love you now. More than I ever thought I could love someone."

Tears blurred her vision but her hearing was still perfect and in every word he spoke she could hear the love for her in his voice. It had always been there, but her insecurities had closed her mind to seeing his love for her.

He kissed away her tears. "Ava, you becoming pregnant had me proposing quicker than I thought I would. But I didn't care. I was so excited to become your husband and a father."

Even though she wanted to believe him, she still needed more. "But why didn't you tell me you loved me? Not once did you say those three little words to me. Why, Cole?"

He shrugged. "I don't know." He held up his hand when she opened her mouth to protest. "Yes, it's a stupid reason but you were the first woman I'd ever loved. The first woman I had such intense feelings for. I didn't know how to handle them. It's not something I'd ever said. I'd seen people saying they loved each other but not meaning the words. I thought if I showed you in everything I did how much I loved you, it would be enough. I guess in this instance, words are stronger than action when it comes to love."

"Yes."

He leaned down and placed a soft, sweet kiss on her lips. Her skin tingled and she wanted to deepen the touch but Cole pulled away. "I'm sorry I didn't tell you, sweetheart. But you need to know, baby or no baby, I'd planned to make you my wife."

"I'm sorry I didn't protect our baby."

"Oh, sweetheart, I don't blame you for losing our baby. Never ever think that."

She nodded and took a deep breath and looked deep into her eyes. "I love you, Cole. I love you with my whole heart."

"I love you too, Ava. With *my* whole heart." He whispered against her lips before capturing them in a kiss full of emotion, hope and joy. Ava returned it with full force, amazed that this handsome man was hers and loved her.

When they broke apart Cole, laid his nose against hers. "There will be no more talk of divorce. We are going to be together for a long, long time."

Tears spilled down her cheeks but she smiled. "Definitely no more talk of divorce. But…" her voice trailed off.

"But what?"

"What about children, Cole? Do you want to try again?"

"I do. I can't think of anything better than seeing my child grow within you. I will let you curse me during labor. And I will be there, walking the hall when our baby is sick or teething." He touched her cheek. "I will do it all, if you want to?"

Ava had no doubt he meant every word he said. Even though it scared her to fall pregnant again, she wanted Cole's baby more than she wanted anything she'd ever wanted before. "Yes. Yes I do."

Cole scooped her up in his arms and carried her to the bed. "Well then, how about we get started tonight?"

"Sounds like a wonderful idea."

As Cole worshipped her body, Ava imagined how their life was going to turn out and she couldn't wait to experience it with Cole. She knew no matter what, Cole would always be by her side and she would always be by his. She had no doubt they'd fight and disagree. But the love they had for each other had endured some difficult times. Their future was going to be wonderful. She couldn't wait to see what tomorrow would bring.

THE END

43304950R00093

Made in the USA
Charleston, SC
19 June 2015